The If Game

'Do you ever play the "If" game? Suppose there's another life going on somewhere where you might have been if something different had happened?'

Stephen's dad doesn't like to play that sort of game. He and Stephen have been alone since Stephen was four, since his mum left—and Dad always refuses to discuss what happened to her.

And then Stephen finds the keys, keys to secret doors that lead him into another world, a world where people he has never seen before seem to know him—and it takes time for him to discover how they are connected with the real world of his present life.

But how can he persuade his father to tell him the truth . . . and will he like what Dad has to say? Maybe it is better not to play the 'If' game after all?

Catherine Storr was born in London and has lived there for most of her life. She always wanted to be a writer, but it wasn't until she was married and had the first two of her three daughters that she had a book published.

When she was feeling despairing of ever being an established writer, she qualified as a doctor and worked for fourteen years in the NHS, writing in the evenings. These stories were written for her various daughters to read. She quickly discovered that she must not tell the stories aloud first, as if she did, she couldn't be bothered to write them. So she had to write in order to discover what happened next. Sadly, Catherine died in January 2001, before publication of *The If Game*, her first book for Oxford University Press.

The If Game

The If Game

Catherine Storr

OXFORD
UNIVERSITY PRESS

OXFORD

UNIVERSITY PRESS

Great Clarendon Street, Oxford OX2 6DP

Oxford University Press is a department of the University of Oxford.
It furthers the University's objective of excellence in research, scholarship,
and education by publishing worldwide in

Oxford New York

Athens Auckland Bangkok Bogotá Buenos Aires Calcutta
Cape Town Chennai Dar es Salaam Delhi Florence Hong Kong Istanbul
Karachi Kuala Lumpur Madrid Melbourne Mexico City Mumbai
Nairobi Paris São Paulo Shanghai Singapore Taipei Tokyo Toronto Warsaw

and associated companies in Berlin Ibadan

Oxford is a registered trade mark of Oxford University Press
in the UK and in certain other countries

British Library Cataloguing in Publication Data available

ISBN 0 19 271873 8

1 3 5 7 9 10 8 6 4 2

Typeset by AFS Image Setters Ltd, Glasgow
Printed and bound in Great Britain by Biddles Ltd
www.biddles.co.uk

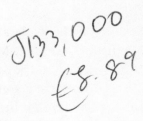

1

Stephen found the keys when he was digging in the garden, something he not often did. That Saturday morning, as they walked through the weekly market, his dad had stopped at the flower stall and unexpectedly bought some plants. He had never, to Stephen's recollection, done this before. In the afternoon, he had offered to double Stephen's pocket money if he'd dig holes for the little rose bushes. Gardening wasn't something that had ever interested Stephen, but he needed the money, so he agreed. It couldn't take long, he thought, and he'd be quite pleased if the boring little plot in front of the house could have some colour in it. Fired by this thought, he bought himself a packet of sweet pea seeds, with a startlingly brilliant picture on the envelope.

There had been a lot of rain. The earth was soft and heavy. He had dug several holes for the little bare brown stems, which didn't look as if they would ever turn into real bushes, and he was whistling a tune he'd heard on the radio, when his spade came up against something hard. A stone probably. But there seemed to be more of it than there was of any of the smallish stones he'd found already. so he dug a little to one side, lifted out a spadeful of earth and saw what it was.

Disappointing. Only an old key.

No. Better than that. More than one key.

When he'd got the objects properly on to his spade and had brushed off some of the clidgy earth, he saw a metal bar, about six inches long, rather like an outsize

1

safety pin, on which were hung three keys of different shapes and sizes.

It wasn't exactly treasure, but it was a lot better than stones. He put them on the weedy path beside the holes.

There is something special about objects you find, even if they are not very interesting in themselves. They are like unexpected presents. You feel they may have possibilities you don't know about. Finding a coin is like this. You don't spend it quite as you would pocket money which you've counted on. He was holding the keys in his hand and whistling again, when a voice from the other side of the fence, said, 'Hi!'

Stephen, startled, said, 'What?'

'I said, "Hi!" I can't see you, but I know you're there.'

The garden next door belonged to Mr Jenkins, who was old and often ill, and who practically never left his house. Stephen had often tried to squint into his garden through holes in the fence, but he'd never been able to see more than a tangle of brambles and the thick, solid leaves of shrubs. This certainly wasn't Mr Jenkins's voice. It was much too young.

'I can't see you, either,' Stephen said.

The voice laughed. Then it said, 'Do you live there?'

'Yes. You don't live with Mr Jenkins, do you?'

'No, *thank* you. I'm here with my mum. Just visiting.'

'Visiting Mr Jenkins?'

'He's my mum's uncle. That's why.'

'What's your name?'

'Alex.'

So it was a boy. Good.

'What's yours?' the voice was saying.

'Stephen.'

'Do you live there with your mum and dad?'

'With my dad.'

'Haven't you got a mum?'

2

Stephen said, 'No,' rather roughly. He hated being asked this question and had never found the right reply.

'I'm sorry,' said the voice. Then it changed and said, 'Sorry! I've got to go. Someone's calling me.' There was a rustle and the sound of twigs snapping. A door slammed. Then silence. Stephen wished he could have seen this Alex. He had quite liked the boy's voice and he had often wished that there was someone living next door who would be more interesting and more fun for him than old Mr Jenkins. He rather hoped that this Alex would come visiting his mum's uncle again. He might invite him into his garden or the house, and then he'd see if he wanted him for a friend.

The questions had made him think about his mum. He had got more or less used at school to fending off questions about her. Sometimes he said, 'She's dead,' which shut people up quickest. Sometimes he said, 'I don't have a mum. I can't even remember her.' If the questions went on after that, he would walk away. Once, Tim Gatley, who was inclined to bully, had gone on and on with stupid questions—'Where had his mum gone?' 'Had she gone off with another bloke?' 'How old had he been when she left?' Finally, Stephen had lashed out and they had had a sort of fight. They had both got bloody noses and sore knees from falling on the asphalt playground, and no one had either lost or won, but from that day Tim hadn't asked any more. Stephen had always had a reputation for a quick temper, and this incident made people even less willing to provoke him.

It was fortunate, Stephen thought, that there were so many people in the school who had single parents. His having only a dad didn't make him peculiar, except for the fact that most of the other singles were mums rather than dads. What did make him different from the rest was that he didn't know anything about his mum. He wasn't even sure that she was dead. When he'd been younger and had asked his dad about her, he'd just been told that she had gone when he was very small, and wouldn't be coming back. 'Did she die?' he had asked, and his dad had said, 'Yes. In a way she's dead.'

At the time, Stephen had taken this to mean that his dad thought they might meet her again in heaven. When he thought about it now, that did not seem a likely explanation, because as far as he knew his dad didn't believe in heaven. But perhaps he did. He never talked about it. He had ended that conversation by saying, 'I don't want to talk about her, Stephen. Don't ask any more.' So he hadn't asked any more. But that was a long time ago. Now that he was growing up, had left primary school and started in the comprehensive, he began to think that he had a right to be told exactly what had happened to her. But it was difficult to start asking again.

While he was thinking this, he had gone indoors, where he washed his find and his black hands. The keys clanked against the side of the sink. He had to scrub them with the vegetable brush to get the encrusted earth out of the patterns on the handles and the flanges.

'What's that?' his dad asked.

'What's what?'

'Something went clink.'

'I found it in the garden. It's only some old keys,' Stephen said.

'What like?' Dad did not sound particularly interested.

Stephen considered, 'One of them's quite big. Got a loop on top.'

'Not one of ours then?'

'Don't think so.'

'If they're no use, get rid of them.'

4

'But they might come in useful.'

'What's a lot of old keys useful for if they don't fit anywhere?'

Stephen said, 'Don't know.'

But any key, however old, must once have had a lock it fitted. He couldn't make up his mind to throw them out just like that. When his hands and the keys were almost dry, he examined them more closely. The largest and most impressive was heavy and solid, made of some metal which he guessed might be brass. It had a square top, pierced with a large hole by which it hung from the metal bar. This top was decorated with what Stephen thought of as squiggles. The stem was ribbed and went down to the flange at the bottom, which was cut into a sort of pattern. It was a handsome piece, and after Stephen had rubbed it with a soft cloth dipped into his dad's metal cleaning tin, it sprang to golden life, shining in the late winter sun as if it had been of gold. Stephen admired it. He wondered what sort of door this key would open. He'd have liked to imagine that it belonged to the gate of a castle. It looked important enough for that.

The second largest key was quite different. It was dark and long and lean, with a smallish loop at its top and a much simpler pattern below. A mean key, he thought, for use, and not for show. Stephen tried polishing it, but it remained black and unpromising. A key for any ordinary door or a shed. He went round the flat trying it in all the keyholes he could find. It was too large for any of the room doors. It did go into the door of the cupboard in the passage, but when Stephen tried to turn it, it got stuck. He had some difficulty getting it out. It was gigantic compared to the locks on the bathroom cabinet and the top drawer of the little chest where his dad kept an assortment of odds and ends. On the rare occasions when this drawer was unlocked and Stephen had looked in, he had seen

5

nothing very interesting. Some very old cigarette cards, a bundle of letters tied in a piece of string, what looked like a photograph album, and a lot of clippings from old newspapers. It had puzzled him that his dad kept the drawer locked. Nothing else in the house was locked, but what he had seen hadn't made him want to examine the drawer's contents more closely.

The third key was an ordinary looking Yale key. But whereas most Yale keys have only one hole in the top, this one had two holes, so that he could imagine it looked up at him out of the kitchen sink like a wicked little shiny face. He thought that Yale keys were boring. This one could have been made for any old door. He took it down to the front door of the house, to make sure it didn't fit there, and it didn't.

It seemed that the keys he had found didn't fit anything. Stephen knew that he ought to throw them away. His dad was always complaining of the junk he hoarded, mostly in cardboard boxes, but he couldn't make up his mind to put the keys in the rubbish bin, just in case. He might, one day, find a use for them. And, anyway, he really liked the big one, with its considerable weight, and its solid top. He could imagine it as one of a bunch of keys worn by—whom? The keeper of a castle? He would have liked to think it was old enough for that. Perhaps it had belonged to a very important man, who had all sorts of secret cupboards and places he had to lock up at night. He liked, too, the little fiddly bits at the end of the key that went into the lock. They looked like a puzzle, perhaps a maze.

He wondered where the keys had come from. How had they come to be buried in the small front garden? He wished he knew their histories, what doors they had opened in the past. He would have liked to get his dad to join him in speculating about them. But Dad didn't like that sort of game. When Stephen said, as he occasionally did, 'What would you do if we won the lottery?' his answer was generally, 'We'd never win, even if I was stupid enough to go in for it.' And when Stephen, much younger, had asked, 'What would you wish for if you had a magic stone that gave you any wish you wanted?' Dad had said 'I'd wish for you to stop asking fool questions.'

So his fantasies would have to be private.

Back in the kitchen, his dad said, 'Still trying out those keys?'

'None of them fit anywhere.'

'You collecting keys or something?' his father asked.

'Not particularly. Why?'

'So? It'd be better than butterflies.'

Stephen sulked. He had once, years ago, thought of collecting butterflies, but after a disastrous experiment with a cabbage white and a really lovely Red Admiral, which made him sick to remember, he had given it up. He could still remember that miserable creature with spoiled wings and a writhing black body which had marked the end to the collection. He had never wanted to try keeping anything live again.

He thought now that perhaps a collection of keys would be possible. He wondered if, perhaps, in a year or two, he would be showing one to an expert, who would say, 'How much did you say you paid for this one? Well, you made a good investment that day. This is one of the very few keys made by . . . ' some unpronounceable name ' . . . and very collectable today. You should insure it for not less than a thousand pounds.'

But, of course, nothing like that would happen.

Stephen thought that if this was the beginning of a proper collection, he should keep his keys in a special place. He would have liked a wooden box with compartments inside. Or, better still, a little chest of tiny drawers. Specimen Chests, they were called. But he hadn't a hope of getting either of those. For want of anything better, he found an old chutney jar with a wide mouth, filled with odds and ends. Trinkets from crackers, half a packet of matches, a whistle that didn't work, a single earring he'd found at school. He emptied them out and, with rare courage, threw them away. Then he made a label saying KEYS and stuck it on the side of the jar.

2

It was a week or two later that the extraordinary thing happened.

It was another Sunday. They'd had their Sunday dinner and Stephen's dad had sat down to watch television. Stephen watched too, for five minutes. Then he lost interest and saw that Dad had too, because his eyes kept closing and soon he had started a gentle snore. Stephen thought perhaps he'd go round to see if Mike was home. They could kick a football around in Mike's garden, which was a lot bigger than Stephen's.

When he found that Mike was out, he was annoyed, and not sure what to do next. He'd have to fill in a lot of time before it began to get dark and he could go home for supper. Then he thought of something he'd been meaning to do for months. He would go to Bridge Street, which was more or less on his way home. Bridge Street backed on to the local railway line, and ended at the railway bridge. It ended in a sharp point, so that the last house in the row must be shaped like a triangle, if, indeed, it had any inside at all. Stephen had an idea that the front of the house, which was just like all the others in the street, wasn't real. He meant, by this, that it wasn't a real house, but was no more than a screen of bricks and pretend windows. A fraud, a forgery, a flim-flam.

Somehow he found this a slightly frightening idea. He didn't like things that looked solid and real and were disguised to hide the fact that they were not. They reminded him of an old historical story he'd read, in which a husband had wanted to get rid of his wife. He had opened the bolts of a trapdoor above a deep shaft in their castle. She had stepped on what she had supposed would be firm ground, and it had given way under her feet and precipitated her down to her death. An oubliette, the device was called, and Stephen never trod on one of those bolted wooden doors set into pavements outside pubs without remembering her and feeling unsafe himself. He felt as if this sham house might conceal the same sort of horror.

When he reached Bridge Street he looked at the front of this house, Number One, with a mixture of fascination and doubt. It could be real. He wished someone would look out of one of the windows, so that he could be sure. But the more he looked, the more it seemed impossible that anyone lived there. The glass in those windows didn't shine in the sun and it was so dim that you couldn't see if there were curtains behind the glass. His eyes fell to the front door, which had been painted when the doors of the sister houses had been painted, but the paint on Number One was dirtier than the others, and the brass knocker had not been polished for years.

As he looked at it, he was overcome by an extraordinary feeling. His heart seemed to give a hop, then to miss a beat, then to knock urgently on his chest wall. At the same time, he felt muzzy. Everything around him seemed to be moving faster than he could understand. He wondered if he could be going to faint. Was this what fainting felt like? Then it passed, and he was standing steadily on the opposite side of the road and gazing at the door. He knew, without a shade of doubt, that he had to go through that door. There was no reason in the feeling, but it was as compulsive as the need to drink when you are parched, or the impulse to hit back if someone attacks you. He crossed over so that he was at the bottom of the three shallow steps leading up to the door. Now he saw that it had a large keyhole. A huge keyhole, like a mouth open to swallow something. He was sure that it was waiting for his key.

He stood there for some time before he turned and went home. Luckily Dad must still be asleep. No voice challenged him as he went across the passage to his room. He took the big key out of the jar and put it in his pocket. Then he began the return journey. He wanted to hurry, as if the big keyhole in the door might disappear. It was when he turned into Bridge Street that he saw the boy.

He was a boy of about his own age, with brown hair, worn rather long, in shabby jeans and an amazing shirt, bright turquoise coloured, with yellow dragons. The sort of shirt Stephen might have admired in a shop window, but which he'd never have had the courage to wear.

When the boy spoke to him, he was surprised. 'Hi!' the boy said.

Stephen said 'Hi!' too, though he didn't like being spoken to by this stranger.

'You're Stephen,' the boy said.

'So what?'

'I'm Alex. Remember? You were in your garden. Weeks ago. We talked through the fence. I was there with my mum. We were visiting her uncle.'

Stephen did remember. 'How did you know me?'

'You came out of next door. And you were whistling the same tune.'

'Holmes, you are wonderful,' Stephen said.

The boy said, 'I wouldn't want to be Sherlock. I'd be Mycroft.'

'Mycroft?'

'He was Sherlock's brother who was cleverer than Sherlock.'

'But you're not either one of them,' Stephen said, and

thought he sounded just like his dad, squashing any sort of play of the imagination.

'I know I'm not. But it doesn't hurt anyone if I think about what I'd be like if things were different. I mean, if I was very rich or one of those people who are brilliant at something like tennis.'

Stephen recognized this as the sort of game he played in his own mind. The wishing game. He said, 'What would you be like?'

'I don't know, do I? It's a sort of game I play with my mum. Don't you ever do it with your dad?'

Stephen said, shortly, 'No, I don't.' He looked up and down the road to show that he meant to be on his way.

'Where are you going?' Alex asked.

'Going to look at a house.' Stephen was not pleased by the question.

'Mind if I come with you?'

'What about your mum? Won't she expect you to be back home?'

'She won't for ages. She's cooking supper for Uncle Joe. It's going to take her years, because she never knows where he's put things, and she has to look all over for them. In funny places.'

Like keys in a chutney jar, Stephen thought. 'What sort of funny places?'

'Last time she wanted to find the tomato sauce, he'd put it in the bathroom.'

'Why?'

'No idea. He couldn't remember. So there's no hurry.'

'Is he crazy?' Stephen asked.

'Not specially. So you see, my mum won't mind. But not if you'd rather I didn't.'

Stephen would very much have rathered that he didn't, but he didn't know how to say so. He said, 'All right. Let's have a look.'

12

As they walked the length of the road, Stephen looked sideways at Alex and tried to guess what he was really like. He couldn't tell much from the face. An ordinary face above an ordinary body. Alex was almost a head shorter than Stephen and a great deal thinner. He had eyes that very slightly slanted upwards at the outer corners, and he seemed to be using them all the time, constantly turning his head this way and that. But he did not speak until they were opposite Number One, Bridge Street. Stephen slowed down.

'Which house did you want to look at?' Alex asked.

'That one.' Stephen pointed.

'Is there something special about it?'

'I can't make out whether it's real or not.'

'What d'you mean, real?'

'It's too thin, see? The way the road slopes off, there isn't room for a proper house. I mean, one that's got a real inside.'

'Let's ring the bell and ask whoever lives there,' Alex said, and before Stephen could stop him, he had leapt across the road and pressed the dim brass bell button beside the door.

Stephen waited to see if any angry householder opened the door. But nothing happened. Rather slowly, he crossed the road and stood beside Alex. Alex pressed the bell again.

'If they catch you . . . ' Stephen said. Alarmed.

'I don't think there's anyone in there,' Alex said.

'I don't think it's a real house,' Stephen said again.

'I wish we could get in, then. I'd like to see the inside that you say isn't really there.'

Stephen hesitated.

'It's a pity we haven't got a key. There's a whopping great keyhole down there,' Alex said.

Stephen didn't want to admit that he had a key that

might fit. Although he still had that urgent feeling that he must open this door, he didn't want to do it with this unknown boy beside him. But the need to know what was the other side of this door was stronger than his reluctance to see it with anyone else. Without speaking, he put his hand into his pocket and took out the key.

'Fantastic! Where'd you get it?' Alex asked.

'Found it.' He wasn't going to explain.

'I like its top. And look at the wards!'

Stephen did not know what he meant. Wards? Like in prisons? He said, 'What about the wards?' Alex put out a finger and touched the key. Stephen realized that 'wards' was the name for the complicated, maze-like shapes on the key which would match whatever lock it had been made for.

'Think it'd fit?' Alex asked.

'Don't know.' He squatted down in front of the door and tried the key in the keyhole. It fitted perfectly and turned as smoothly as if the lock had been oiled.

'What's the matter?' Alex asked, as Stephen still hesitated.

'I'm not sure there'll be anything inside.'

'You won't find out unless you look,' Alex said, and without waiting, he pushed the door open. Stephen was standing inside before he'd had time to think.

3

Stephen was astonished to see what looked like a path leading away from where he stood. A long path. He hadn't supposed there could be anything like so much space between the front of the house and the back, which overlooked the railway line below. He took a step forward and stood inside the open door. Then, impelled by curiosity, he walked a yard or so further.

The door suddenly banged shut behind him. He turned, and saw that Alex wasn't with him. He must have been shut out. Perhaps it had been Alex who had shut the door and had purposely stayed outside. Stephen was annoyed. It had been Alex who had egged him on to enter this house, and now had left him alone to face whatever it contained.

He looked around. He was relieved that no one appeared to ask him what he was doing there, or to complain that he was trespassing. It was very odd. What was still odder was the length of the path before him. He had always thought of this house as being nothing but a front wall. He knew, or thought he did, that the angle at which the roads met at the railway bridge must mean that there was no room for a proper house to exist; and yet, here he was, apparently inside it, with the path leading away into the distance. And, stranger still, it wasn't a passage inside a house, it was an outdoor path with fences each side and trees overhanging the fences. There was grass growing at the bottom of the fences and little climbing plants clinging to the wood. The trees were unfamiliar. They were tall and they still had all their leaves, of an unfamiliar bluish green, and what was even more extraordinary, Stephen realized that he was far too hot, as if it was summer instead of the middle of winter. He thought that the front door must have opened directly into the glasshouse of the sham house's garden. That made sense. But if there was not room for a real house, how could there be room for a garden of the size that this one appeared to be? He had never noticed, from the train windows, anything like a garden just here. To find out how he could have been so mistaken, he moved forward along the path.

There were benches between the fences and the path, and on one of them, just ahead, an old man was sitting, with a newspaper in his hands, which he was looking at without much interest. Stephen wondered if he could ask him how there came to be so much space behind the sham house, and as he approached the bench, he slowed down. The old man lifted his head and looked at Stephen. He smiled as if they knew each other, though Stephen wasn't aware that they'd ever met. He said, 'Back already?'

'Back?' Stephen said, puzzled.

'You've not been long gone.'

'Where from?' Stephen asked, confused. The conversation didn't seem to make sense.

'From your aunt's. I thought you were staying for tea.'

It was clear that he'd been mistaken for someone else. Stephen said, 'I don't think you do really know me.'

'Weren't you going to your aunt's? Someone said you were.'

'No, I wasn't,' Stephen said. He never went to see Aunt Alice by himself. He went sometimes, unwillingly, with Dad.

The old man suddenly grew angry. 'Don't you try to trick me! I may be old and forget things sometimes, but I know you were going there.'

16

The old man must be mad. Stephen said, 'I think you've made a mistake. Perhaps I look like someone you know.'

The old man became angrier still. 'Don't tell me I don't know you! I've known you since you were so high.' His hand indicated the height of a small child.

'All right! Who am I then?' Stephen said.

He was expecting the old man to come up with some name he'd never heard of. But the old man did not answer. Instead, he said, 'Now, stop this nonsense and come back home.' He got slowly up from the bench and began to walk along the path away from the house.

Stephen did not follow him. He said, 'I don't know you, and you don't know me.' It seemed important to make this clear, to get the old man to agree that some monstrous mistake was being made.

The old man turned back and took Stephen's sleeve and began trying to pull Stephen to go with him. He was surprisingly strong and Stephen had to dig his heels in to resist him. He had no intention of getting caught up in the web of the old man's imagination. Finally, after they had wrestled for a short time, neither of them gaining any ground, Stephen succeeded in tearing his sleeve from the man's grasp. He did it so violently that he felt the sleeve rip, and the old man tottered and fell back on to the bench he'd been sitting on. Stephen had a moment's fear that he was really hurt, but he wasn't going to risk being caught again. He turned back towards the house and he ran. Before him, he saw the other side of the house, as flat and unreal as its front had been. But there was the door through which he'd come to this strange place. He still had the big key in his hand. He forced it into the keyhole, turned it and the door opened. He almost fell through.

4

He looked at the road below him and was grateful for its ordinariness. He also saw Alex, apparently waiting for him. He was not pleased. He did not feel ready to talk to anyone about the disturbing experience he had just had.

'Well?' Alex said.

'Well what?'

'What is it like in there? Is there any house?'

'No.'

'Just a drop down to the railway line?'

'Not exactly. There's a sort of path.' He wasn't going to explain how long and unlikely that path had been.

'You don't sound as if you liked it.'

Stephen said, 'I didn't.'

'What's wrong with it?'

'I don't know. It's . . . funny.'

'Funny ha-ha? Or just peculiar?'

'Peculiar,' Stephen said. He had no words to describe how peculiar it had seemed. First, there being a long straight path were there should only have been the falling ground above the railway line, and second, the old man who had mistaken him for someone else.

He had turned to walk home and found that Alex was walking beside him. He wasn't best pleased by this, but as the boy was there, he thought he might as well try to get some reassurance from him. He said, 'Do people often have doubles?'

'Doubles how? What do you mean by doubles?'

'Other people who look exactly like them.'

'When they're not twins, you mean? Twins can look exactly like each other.'

'When they're not twins.' But a horrible thought now struck Stephen. Suppose, without knowing it, he had a twin? Since you can't remember being born, how would you know, if your parents didn't tell you? He had read somewhere a story which he'd always found upsetting, about a man who thought he was seeing himself in a mirror, but had really seen a twin brother he'd never heard of, on the other side of a glass door. It was a spooky story which had haunted him for weeks after reading it.

'I've no idea,' Alex was saying. It took Stephen a moment to realize that this was an answer to his question. Alex went on, 'I know we're all supposed to have a double somewhere else in the world. But it would have to be around where we live, wouldn't it? I mean, we couldn't have a double in China. Or Africa. Or anywhere where people don't look anything like us.'

Was that comforting? Or not? Stephen didn't know.

'Why do you want to know? Did you meet your double the other side of that door?' Alex asked, and Stephen, taken by surprise, cried out, 'No!' so loudly that people passing them in the street turned to look at him.

'It's all right. You don't need to shout. I didn't say you did,' Alex said.

'I didn't, anyway.'

'Something happened, though. Didn't it?' Alex asked.

'Why?'

'You're upset. As if you didn't like whatever it was.'

Stephen was not going to tell him anything. He wanted to get rid of Alex. He said, 'Why don't you go home?'

'You mean you don't want me with you?' Alex asked, and Stephen, who wasn't usually as rude as this, said, 'No, I don't.'

Alex turned red. He said, 'I don't want to be with you, either,' and turned away. Stephen, feeling bad, said, 'I didn't mean . . . ' but Alex was out of hearing, or pretending that he hadn't heard. Either way suited Stephen. He needed to be by himself. They were just at the point where Bridge Street crossed the High Street, so he turned into the High Street instead of continuing directly towards his home street. As he'd hoped, Alex went straight on towards his uncle's house, without saying another word.

Stephen went into the nearest newspaper shop and bought himself a magazine. When he thought that he'd given Alex time to get indoors he also went home.

His dad was sitting in the kitchen, sipping a cup of tea and reading the paper. Stephen felt the teapot, found it was still more hot than warm, and poured himself out a mug of only slightly stewed tea. He reached for a biscuit from the red tin which held sweet biscuits—the savoury biscuits were in a round green tin—and waited. He knew by experience that it was no good asking Dad an important question while he was engrossed in the paper. He wouldn't get a serious answer.

It seemed that he had waited a long time before Dad began folding the paper in the way that meant he'd read almost all he wanted. Then Stephen began.

'Dad.'

'What?'

He didn't know how to ask. It would sound so funny. He wished he could find some way of leading into the subject, but he couldn't think of anything. He said, 'Dad, was I a twin?'

'A what?'

'Was I one of twins when I was born?'

His dad was scornful. 'You, a twin? No! Whatever made you think that up?'

'Someone I was talking to today was talking about doubles. Said lots of people have them.'

'First I've heard of it. There being many of them. Doesn't seem sense.'

'But there could be doubles? I mean, there could be someone who looked exactly like me. Somewhere.'

'Let me know when you see him,' Dad said, uninterested, and opened his paper again.

Stephen was relieved to know that he hadn't got a twin somewhere or other. It would have been an uncomfortable feeling. He considered the idea that Dad hadn't told him the truth, but he had to dismiss it instantly. Dad was difficult, liked his own way, could be maddeningly silent, wouldn't argue, never expressed any feelings, but he wasn't a liar. Then he thought about the old man. He decided that the old man was confused, as old men sometimes are. Probably Stephen looked like a boy he knew, which wasn't unlikely. Stephen could think of several other boys at his school who weren't very different to look at. It was quite possible to mistake one for another, especially when they all wore much the same sort of clothes. And probably the old man's sight wasn't good. Had he been wearing spectacles? Stephen thought not. He consoled himself by thoughts along these lines. All the same it had been a nasty experience. He hoped he wouldn't meet that man again.

'Who was it told you about doubles?' Dad's voice interrupted his musings.

'Alex. The boy next door.'

'What boy next door?'

'He doesn't live there. His mum's Mr Jenkins's niece. I was talking to him through the fence one day, and then I met him again this afternoon, in the street.'

Dad laughed.

'What are you laughing at, Dad?'

'Because you've got it wrong. It isn't a boy. It's a girl.'

J/33, 000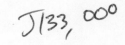

Stephen stared. 'He can't be! He doesn't look like a girl!' But didn't he? It was true that Alex's hair was rather long, but a lot of boys now had quite long hair, and most of the girls he knew wore trousers as often as skirts.

'So you've seen her? As well as spoken through the fence?' his dad was saying.

'Saw him this afternoon. Are you sure? I mean . . . is he really a girl?'

'That's what her mum says, and she ought to know.'

Stephen didn't know what he was feeling. Annoyed, furious even, that he'd been taken in. He'd talked to Alex as if she'd been a boy, an equal. If he'd known she was a girl, he wouldn't have talked like that. He wasn't sure what difference it would have made, but still, he felt cheated. He also felt that if she was only a girl, he needn't take anything she said seriously.

'You don't look pleased,' his dad said.

Stephen didn't answer this.

'I don't see that it makes that much difference. If you liked her when you thought she was a boy.'

'I didn't say I liked her.'

'Anyway, you don't have to see her again if you don't want,' his dad said.

'I shan't. Ever,' Stephen said.

'We'll be having supper in half an hour. About,' his dad said.

Stephen said, 'Right.'

But he was no longer hungry. He was more upset than he could explain to himself. He had somehow lost dignity by being involved with a girl. If he met her again, he'd pretend not to know her. At the back of his mind there was also a faint regret that he'd lost a possible friend. He'd thought of things that the boy Alex and he could do together. He certainly wasn't going to make a friend of a miserable girl.

5

Stephen never knew for certain how Sundays were going to turn out. There were black Sundays, when he and Dad had to visit Dad's mother, Stephen's gran. This was something neither of them enjoyed, and the thought of what they were going to do in the afternoon made the mornings heavy and depressing. But on this particular Sunday, which was unexpectedly fine after a horribly wet week, after Stephen's dad had written the letter which occupied most of his Sunday mornings, he wanted to go for what he called their country walk. It wasn't quite real country, you were never out of sight of the town's chimneys and tall blocks, but the lane soon left its bordering houses behind, and wandered up and down small hills as it had done ever since it had been the path along which shepherds drove their sheep and, perhaps, geese, which were taken to the goose fair, miles away, walking in little web-shaped shoes, made for them by kind shoemakers out of soft leather left over from proper people's footwear. It was still muddy, and was bounded on one side by a hedge, and on the other by ragged trees, which now had fat green and brown buds and the beginnings of leaves.

'Smells like spring,' Stephen's dad said.

'You can't smell spring,' Stephen said, wanting vaguely to be disagreeable. He was bored with this walk. They did it too often and it annoyed him that his dad liked it.

'You may not be able to, but I can,' his dad said.

'And it's not proper country here.'

23

'It's the best we've got.'

'I wish we could live right out in the country. Or by the sea. Miles from anywhere.'

'Oh yes? And where'd you go to school? And where would I get work?'

'I could fish. And we could grow vegetables and sell what we didn't want for ourselves.'

'Sounds fine, but I don't think we'd better try it just yet.'

'Why not?' But he knew, quite well, why not. They hadn't got enough money to buy a cottage in the country or by the sea. They had just enough to stay where they were, in a flat that didn't cost much because it was dark and dilapidated, where the garden wasn't much bigger than the headmaster's study at school, and which was near enough for them to walk to their daytime occupations. Stephen to school and Dad to the garage where he worked.

After the usual Sunday midday meal, scrambled eggs on toasted cheese and sausages, Dad sat down with his paper in front of the television. Stephen sat too, until he could forget the full feeling in his stomach. Then he went to his own room and sat on the side of the bed in order to think.

He looked at the jar which held the three keys and he wondered. The big one, what he thought of as 'the castle key', had opened the door of that mysterious non-house. He wondered if he'd go back and see if the path was really there, or if, as he'd expected, there would be nothing but the railway embankment.

He wondered if he could have dreamed that encounter with the old man. He thought not. After all, he'd met Alex again immediately afterwards and he hadn't felt sleepy. It had all seemed absolutely real. And it was possible that he'd been mistaken in thinking that there couldn't be any ground behind the house. There really had been a path and he'd walked along it. It must have been the garden of the house. He knew he ought to go back and look again, but for some reason he was extremely unwilling to do this. So he continued to sit on his bed and try to invent reasons for what had happened. At last, he decided that the only sensible thing to do was to ask Dad again about the possibility of there being someone who looked like him.

He would have to wait for just the right moment. If Dad was thinking about something else, or was in a hurry, there was no way he'd ever answer a question which didn't seem to him important. But the moment seemed to have come that evening, when they were sitting together in the kitchen, having had their supper, waiting for the television programme they both enjoyed. Stephen summoned his courage and began.

'Dad?'

'What?'

'Aunt Alice is the only aunt I've got, isn't she? There aren't any more?'

His dad sat up suddenly and looked across the table at him in a way that Stephen didn't like. As if he'd done something dreadful.

'What makes you ask that?' Dad said.

'I just wondered. Because of something someone said.'

'Who said?' Dad asked.

'No one. I mean, there was an old man . . . '

'Where? Who?'

'I met him. On a bench.'

'Round here, was it?'

Stephen didn't know how he could explain. He said, 'Along Bridge Street.'

'What did he tell you?'

'He didn't tell me anything. He thought I knew people he knew. He talked about someone being my aunt.'

'Did he say what she was called?'

25

'No.'

'What sort of man? What did he look like?'

'Old. White hair.'

'How old? Tall or short? What did he say?'

'He seemed as if he thought he knew me. But I've never seen him before. But I don't know him, do I?'

'No, you don't. What else?'

'Nothing else. I got away.'

'He didn't say his name?'

'No.'

Dad sat silent for a moment or two. Then he said, 'Did he seem to be looking for you?'

'No. He was just there when I came up to where he was sitting and then he said, "Back already?" as if he'd been expecting me.'

'He didn't say back from where?'

'That's when he said about an aunt. He thought I'd been to see her.'

'Did he know your name?'

'He didn't say so. But if he thought I belonged to his family, he wouldn't have to say it, would he?'

Stephen could see that Dad was upset. 'Tell me exactly what this man looked like. Old, you said?'

'Not very. Like I said, he had white hair. Not a lot of it.'

'He didn't say who he was?'

'He thought I knew. It was really weird.'

What was just as weird was the way Dad was taking this. Stephen could see that he was worried. Stephen said, 'That's why I was asking you about twins.'

'Twins? What are you talking about?'

'When I got back from being out that day. I asked you if I could ever have had a twin. I thought perhaps there was someone who looked exactly like me and that was why he picked on me.'

26

'When was that? I'd forgotten.'

'Couple of weeks ago.'

'And you haven't seen him again since then?'

'No.'

'No one's written to you?'

'No.' This was really puzzling. Why should Dad think that anyone would write to him? Stephen never got letters. An occasional—very occasional—picture postcard from a school friend away on holiday was all the post he ever got.

'Where did you say you saw this man?'

'Near Bridge Street.'

'In the street, was it? He didn't ask you in anywhere?'

Stephen hesitated a moment before he said, 'Yes, out of doors.' It had been out of doors, even though he'd expected that door to lead into a house. Dad didn't appear to notice the hesitation. He said, 'If you see that man again, Stephen, don't talk to him. If he tries to get talking to you, just walk away and leave him be.'

'D'you think he's dangerous?' Stephen asked.

'Not exactly. But I don't want you to have anything to do with him.'

'Do you know who he is, then? Is he a murderer? Or what?' Stephen's vivid imagination had already cast the man as a child abductor. Perhaps a dangerous lunatic, who shouldn't really be out on the streets. Whatever he was, he found it exciting as well as scary. He said, 'Dad, I'm not a baby. You don't think I'd go off with someone just because they asked?'

'No. Well, don't. That's all.'

'But if you think he's dangerous, shouldn't we tell the police?'

'I didn't say he was dangerous. It's just . . . I don't think he's someone you should know.'

'You know him, though, don't you?' Stephen asked.

Dad didn't answer. Stephen was used to Dad's not answering questions. He felt sure that Dad must know the old man. So what was wrong with him? Why was Dad upset about him?

That evening he was intrigued to see Dad writing a letter. He suspected that this was something to do with the incident with the old man. Dad wrote quite a few letters, one every Sunday, but Stephen never knew whom he wrote to, and if he asked, he was never told. Dad always took the letters to post himself, Stephen never had sight of the envelopes. Generally he wrote quite fast, but this letter seemed to be giving him trouble. He kept on stopping, and looking round the room, scratching his head and sighing. It was a short letter, not near as long as those he ordinarily wrote. He didn't address the envelope straight off, either. He had to go to his room first. To look up the address, Stephen guessed. Could he be writing to the police? It was all very mysterious. It was also annoying. Dad was treating him like a small child, afraid that he was in danger of being abducted by a stranger. Stephen's dignity was insulted. He was sure he could look after himself.

6

In spite of his dad's warnings, Stephen spent quite a lot of time during the next few weeks looking around to see if he could find the old man again. But he never caught sight of him or of anyone like him, and as time went on, his interest in the mystery waned. He was also looking around whenever he was out in the town in case he saw Alex, whom he would have chosen to avoid. It was just his bad luck that one Saturday morning, as he came out on to the road from his own house, she was coming out from next door. It was impossible to pretend that they hadn't seen each other. They were almost face to face. Stephen felt horrible. Not only because he knew he'd been unprovokedly rude at their last meeting, but more, because he'd mistaken her for a boy. Had he said anything in their brief conversation which could have told her of his mistake? That would be unbearably embarrassing.

He saw that she had turned red. Perhaps she was going to pay him back for telling her that he didn't want her company. But instead she said, 'Hi!', and it was guarded but not unfriendly.

Stephen hoped that she might have forgotten their last meeting. He also said, 'Hi!'

'You still cross with me?' she asked.

'No.' To his surprise, he found he wasn't. It wasn't her fault that he'd thought of her as a boy.

'You were last time we met. Outside that funny house you wanted to go into.'

He wouldn't admit it, so he said, 'Well, I'm not now.'

'I'm just going to get my mum's paper,' she said. The post office, which sold newspapers, was in the opposite direction from where Stephen meant to go. Gratefully, he said, 'I've got to go this way.' He certainly didn't want her hanging around again.

'Bye then,' she said and was off.

Not too bad, he thought. She could have been really fed up with the way he'd spoken to her after that odd experience in the sham house. He went to Dan's house and found Mike already there. They kicked a ball around for a bit, but it wasn't the same as having enough people for two proper teams. Stephen left them and went to the library to see if there were any books he might want to read, but he found it difficult to choose anything that interested him for more than half an hour or so. He almost wished that the short Easter holiday was over already. He was surprised to find, a week later, that he was quite pleased when the summer term started, and he was back at school. Time could drag there, but the clock didn't seem to go anything like as slowly as at home.

The weather changed for the better, too. After a miserably cold, wet April, the sun came out and the wind blew softly. One Saturday, walking back from visiting Mike, he found himself in a street he didn't know well, one side of a square of rather elegant houses. There were little pillars, supporting small balconies over the front doors, and the tops of the ground floor windows were arched. There were brick walls separating the houses. Stephen supposed that behind these were the houses' gardens. He was strolling along, admiring the houses and wishing he and his dad lived in something as nice to look at, when he suddenly stopped. He felt muzzy, and his heart seemed to be beating twice as fast as it should. He had had this feeling before and now he knew what it was.

He looked around. Opposite to him was a green garden door, set in one of the walls. With a sinking of the heart, he realized that this was one of the doors he had to go through.

But how could he just walk into someone's garden? He crossed the road and examined the door. It had a large round wooden handle, and he tried it, but though it turned, the door did not open. Indeed, above the handle was a keyhole.

It was a keyhole for a Yale key. And Stephen had a Yale key, one of the three he had found in the garden. It was in his room at home, but he did not hesitate. He went back to the flat, took the key out of the chutney jar and ran back to the door in the wall.

When he was back in the square, he tried to consider what would be the best way of getting through that door. He could, of course, simply try his key in the door, and if it opened, just walk in. But he was unwilling to do that. He looked at the front door of the house to which he supposed the garden belonged, and wondered whether to ring the bell and ask if he might have a look at the garden. No. He couldn't do that. They'd think he was crazy. He decided that it would be better to use his key and open the door, and if anyone challenged him, he would say that it was all a mistake, he'd lost his way and thought that this was his garden. It sounded an unlikely story, but he couldn't think of anything better. So he inserted the key in the lock. It turned and when he also used the wooden handle the door swung inwards.

Stephen looked cautiously through the gap. He saw the garden he'd expected. It was large and green and seemed full of people, all talking. They were sitting round a big table spread with food. But as he looked, the talking died down and all heads were turned towards him. He was acutely embarrassed.

He said, 'I'm sorry. I just wanted to know what was here.' He half expected to be told to go away quickly, or even to be told he had no business to open a door into an unknown garden. Instead of this, a woman got up from the table and came towards him. She was smiling.

'Well, come in, now you're here,' she said. Her hand was on his shoulder and she was pushing him towards the table. 'Just in time. Chris hasn't cut the cake yet.'

Stephen saw now that on the table there was a large iced cake, with candles. Behind it was a small boy with curly brown hair. He said, 'I'm going to cut it now!' and flourished a knife. A voice called out, 'Blow out the candles first!'

The boy took a deep breath and blew. All the candles but one went out. Someone leaned forward and pinched it so that the little flame disappeared.

'Now cut it!' someone said.

'But you must wish!' a woman said.

The boy said, 'I'm going to.'

'You mustn't tell us what it is,' another voice said.

The boy, Chris, said, 'Shan't tell anyone.' He plunged the knife into the cake, but to cut a slice was more than he could manage. The woman who had told him to wish was beside him, and she held his hand and guided the knife so that the pieces of cake, which were more like mounds of crumbs than slices, could be piled on a plate.

Stephen expected that at any moment someone would realize that he had no right to be there. But the woman who had pushed him towards the table, handed the plate to him as he approached where they were standing. 'Go on, it's good,' she said, and Stephen, not knowing how to refuse, took the smallest slice he could see. She was right. It was good.

'I'm sorry. I didn't mean to barge in,' he said, his mouth full of cake.

32

'You didn't barge in. Didn't you get the invitation?' she asked, also through a mouthful of crumbs. He didn't know how to answer that. Of course he hadn't had an invitation to the birthday of someone he'd never met before. He looked round at the other guests to see if there could be anyone there whom he knew, who might have invited him. But they were all strangers. Not only strangers, but something about the way they spoke made him think that they were not English. They had a curious accent which he couldn't name, and yet they talked as if English were their native tongue. American perhaps?

'I know Chris asked for you to come,' the woman said.

Stephen felt acutely uncomfortable. Here he was again, with people who seemed to know him, though he had no idea who they were. He said, 'I think there's been a mistake. I didn't really mean to come to his party . . . '

But she interrupted him. 'Just because you didn't like what Rose said the other day? You shouldn't hold it against Chris. It wasn't anything to do with him.'

More confusing than ever. Stephen said, 'Who's Rose?'

The woman stared. 'Rose. You know Rose,' she said.

'No. I don't. Look! It's all a mistake. I shouldn't have come in here. I don't know any of you. I don't know Rose and I've never seen you before.'

'There's no need to take it like that. Calm down, won't you?' the woman said.

'I'm quite calm,' Stephen said. It wasn't true. He was angry and frightened. He didn't know what was going on. It seemed as if there were people around who were out to confuse him, to pretend that he was someone he wasn't. He said, 'All right, if you think I know you, tell me who I am. You don't even know my name.'

'Not know you? I've known you since you were a baby.

You're Deedie,' the woman said. She turned round to address the rest of the company. 'Here's Deedie, playing the usual games, pretending he doesn't know us. What do you think of that?'

Stephen had the impression that the people seated round the table were all standing up and staring at him, with angry eyes. But he didn't wait to see more. Shaken to the core, he turned and ran for the door in the wall. The key was still in his hand. He pushed it into the keyhole, turned the wooden knob and, to his relief, found himself on the pavement outside.

7

Stephen went home, disturbed. It seemed that here, in the town he'd lived in all his life, there were people who thought they knew him, whom he was supposed to know. It had been bad enough when it was only the old man. He could explain that to himself as a mistake made by an old man's failing eyesight. But the people today hadn't been old and there were several of them. Worse, and more puzzling still, they had known his name. Not his name today, but the name he'd been called by when he was very young and couldn't pronounce 'Stephen' himself. It was enough to make him feel dizzy, without the extra pressure of the feelings he had when he saw a door and knew he had to go through it.

There must be some sensible explanation. He would have to tackle Dad, and that needed courage. Dad hated to be asked questions and generally managed not to answer them. Stephen considered. He tried all sorts of explanations of what had happened, but they all seemed ridiculous and impossible, until the great idea suddenly struck him. This would account for everything, even Dad's attitude. That evening he waited until the meal was over, but before Dad could get interested in any of the television programmes or start reading the paper again, Stephen said, 'Dad! I want to ask you something.'

His dad pushed his chair back from the table and said, 'Go on, then.'

'Did you adopt me?'

He saw at once that the answer would be 'No'. His

35

dad's face expressed utter astonishment. He said, 'What on earth put that idea into your head?'

'I told you about the old man who thought he knew me?'

'You haven't seen him again?'

'No. But I met some other people, and they thought they knew me, too.'

'What sort of people?'

'I don't know. A lot of women.'

'What did they tell you?' Dad asked.

'They didn't tell me anything. They just seemed to think I knew them. So I thought perhaps you'd adopted me and there was someone from wherever I came from who looked just like me. Like a twin.'

'I did not adopt you and you never had a twin,' Dad said.

'It's funny, then. I don't mean that sort of funny. I don't like it.'

Dad was silent for a time. Then he said, 'When you say they seemed to know you, what did they say?'

'They talked as if I'd been invited to the party.'

'What party? You didn't say a party.'

'A birthday party. For the little boy.'

'You didn't say a little boy, either.'

'He was called Chris. They seemed to think I knew all about them.'

Dad thought. 'Was that man there? The one you said started talking to you.'

'Ages ago, you mean? No, he wasn't.'

'These other people. What did they look like?'

Difficult. He hadn't really looked at them carefully. He said, 'Ordinary. But they knew my name. What it used to be.'

'What d'you mean, "used to be"?'

'They said Deedie. One of the women said she'd known

me since I was a baby. But I don't know her. I've never seen her before in my life. Not that I can remember, anyway.'

Dad's face was serious, even severe. He did not speak.

'Who are they, Dad? You know, don't you?'

Dad seemed to be having difficulty speaking. He swallowed once or twice. Then he said, 'Show me where this happened.'

Stephen did not want to have to admit that he had opened a door into a private garden. But with Dad looking like that, he had no chance of refusing. He said, 'All right. When d'you want . . . ?'

'Now,' his dad said, in a voice like a hammer blow. Dad got up and reached for his stick. That was odd. He very seldom walked with his stick. He didn't speak again, but made for the front door. Stephen, unwilling, followed.

Out in the street he had to take the lead. He walked as slowly as he thought Dad would bear. He was not looking forward to going back into that garden and seeing all the people who thought they knew him, but who were strangers. Especially with his dad in this savage mood. Several times Dad said, 'Get a move on, can't you?', and even once or twice pushed him to try to hurry him up. At last they reached the square with the elegant houses. Dad looked around, surprised. 'Here?' he said, and Stephen said, 'Yes, here.'

'Which house?' Dad asked.

'It wasn't in a house. It was a garden. There,' Stephen said, pointing to the door in the brick wall.

'How'd you get in? There's no bell here,' Dad said.

'I had a key that worked,' Stephen said.

'And you just walked in? Like that?'

'I didn't think the key would fit. I just wanted to try it,' Stephen said.

37

'Got the key now?'

He wished he hadn't. Why hadn't he thought of leaving it at home? The affair was becoming too embarrassing. But he said that, yes, he had got the key.

'Go on, then. Let's see,' Dad said.

Stephen produced the Yale key. He put it in the door. It did not turn.

'Sure it was this door?'

He was quite sure.

'Let me try that key,' Dad said. But the key in his hand did not turn in the lock when he tried it, any more than it had in Stephen's. 'Can't have been this door. Must be one of the others,' he said, standing back from the wall and looking up and down the road. 'There's plenty of other doors like this one,' he said.

Stephen didn't know whether to insist that it had been this one and no other. He saw that Dad didn't mean to give up, so he said, 'All right. Let's try the others.'

Altogether there were fifteen doors of the same kind, set into the brick walls beside the house fronts. There were seven on one side of the square and eight on the other. They couldn't try them all, because many hadn't got Yale locks. But they did try Stephen's key in about half of them and it did not fit any one. By the end of the exertion, Stephen was red with embarrassment, and his dad was angry.

'You sure it was this road?' he asked.

'Certain.'

'We'll go back and try that first one again,' Dad said. But the key still didn't turn in the lock. 'Sure you've brought the same key with you?' Dad asked.

'I haven't got another one anything like it,' Stephen said.

'Then we'll have to ask at the door,' Dad said. Stephen had no idea what he meant, till he saw his dad walk up

38

to the front door of the house next to the garden wall. He cried out, 'No! Don't!' but it was too late. Dad had already rung the bell.

Stephen waited for the door to open and for his dad to try to explain. He would have liked to walk away but he knew Dad wouldn't stand for that. He expected someone from inside that elegant house to shout that no one was allowed into the private garden and that it must be nonsense that he could have a key that fitted. Now that the key no longer turned in the lock, he had no evidence to prove his story. Perhaps the house owner would call the police and then what would Dad say?

He need not have worried. The front door did not open. Dad rang the bell again. A woman came out of the next door house, with a pushchair containing a large, solemn baby. She let it carefully down the front three steps, and when she was on the pavement, she said to Dad, 'Did you want to speak to Mrs . . . ?' Stephen didn't catch the name. 'I'm afraid she's not there. There's nobody there. The family left in the spring and the house has been on the market ever since.'

Stephen heard his dad say, 'Left last spring?'

'That's right. The agents can't sell it. They say the price is way too high. It's the gardens. They're very big for this part of the town. They're wonderful for children.' As she spoke, she looked down into the pushchair, as if she were reminded that this was what her garden was for. She smiled, and Stephen saw the baby's fat serious face crinkle up into an answering, toothless grin. He looked away. He was disturbed. If he had been able to put his feelings into words, he would have asked a question. 'Is that how babies feel about their mothers? Is that how mothers feel about their babies?'

'So there wouldn't have been anyone here this afternoon?' Dad asked.

'Not unless it was the agents showing someone round.'

Dad said, 'Thanks for telling me.' Then he said, 'Which garden belongs to which house here? That one over there, does it go with this house?' He pointed to the brick wall with the door Stephen had gone through.

'That's right. All the gardens this side of the square are on the right hand side of the houses they go with. This is ours,' she said, nodding her head towards the wall behind her.

Dad was saying, 'Thanks', and then, impatiently, to Stephen, 'Come on. Let's get back.' He had already started walking away. Stephen followed him. He wondered how Dad was going to explain away this last piece of information.

As they walked, Dad said, 'Can't have been that garden. You must have got the street wrong.'

Stephen said nothing. He couldn't explain what he thought had happened. There was no point in arguing. If Dad could be convinced that the whole thing had been a mistake, that was the best he could hope for. Nothing more was said between them until they were back inside their own front door.

8

Stephen had known before they had reached home that his dad wasn't going to leave things there. He was sure there had to be more questions and more demands for an explanation to come, and he wanted some of the explanations for himself. Dad was not to be the only person who asked questions. Dad began.

'I want to get this clear, Stephen. The people you say you saw in that garden—never mind where it is exactly—what did they say? What did they tell you?'

'I've said already, they didn't tell me anything. They thought they knew me, that's all.'

'They called you Deedie?'

'One of them did.'

'Did they say any other names?'

'The boy was called Chris. I told you that.'

'Nothing else?'

'One of them said something about Rose.'

Stephen saw that this startled Dad. He sat up straight and his voice was different when he said, 'Rose? You sure?'

'They thought I knew her,' Stephen said.

'They didn't talk about anyone else?'

'No. And I don't think they believed me when I said I didn't know anyone called Rose.'

Dad took a long deep breath. Stephen thought he might be going to say something more, but he didn't. He just sat there, looking down at the table without speaking.

The silence grew uncomfortable. Stephen said, 'I wish you'd tell me what it's all about.'

'What what's all about?'

'You know who they are, don't you? Like the time I saw that old man, and you said not to have anything to do with him. Why don't you tell me who he is and what's happening.'

Dad did not reply at once. After another long pause he said, 'From what you say, I think they're a family I used to know. But I don't now. And I don't want to, and I don't want you to know them either.'

'Why not?' Stephen asked.

'Never mind why not. I just don't think they'd be any good for you, that's all.'

'Are they something to do with my mum?' Stephen asked. This would explain why Dad seemed so upset, he thought. It was a brave question. He had hardly ever asked Dad direct questions about his mother. He knew that Dad didn't like those questions he had asked in the past and he was risking an outburst of anger now.

'Your mum knew them, if they're who I think they are,' Dad said.

'You mean they were friends of hers? Of her family?'

'Sort of,' Dad said.

'What's happened to her family?'

'What do you mean, what's happened?'

'Why don't we ever see them? I mean, we see your mum and Aunt Alice, but I've never seen my mum's mum. Or anyone.'

'That's because they don't live in this country.'

'Where are they, then?' Stephen asked. He could feel that his dad was edgy. Probably wouldn't answer many more questions.

'They're the other side of the world,' Stephen's dad said in the voice that meant 'and that's the end of this conversation.'

But he persisted. 'Did my mum come from wherever that is?'

'No, she didn't. Stephen, I've told you, I don't want to talk about her.'

'I only want—'

He was interrupted. His dad said, 'And I don't want. If you've finished your supper, I suggest you get on with your homework.'

'I haven't got any. It's half term.'

'You can help clear the table, then. And then you can go and read something, or watch the telly. Don't come plaguing me with questions.'

Stephen helped clear the table and wash the dishes. He saw his dad immerse himself in the evening paper and he turned on the television. For a time he watched a quiz programme which didn't much interest him, because he didn't know the answers to any of the questions. He saw his dad put down the paper and watch too. The quiz programme was followed by the news, which Stephen found equally boring.

He sat in front of the television screen, his eyes open but without attending to a word. He was trying to summon up enough courage to risk his dad's anger. Before this he had always stopped questioning when he was told to, but this time he wouldn't. He waited until the next day's weather had been forecast, and then said, 'Dad?'

'What?'

'I know you don't like me asking, but I think it's time I knew. About my mum.'

'I told you, I don't want to talk about her.'

'I've a right to know. Whatever it is you don't want to talk about.'

'You're old enough to understand that when I say I'm not going to tell you any more, that's it.'

43

'You can't tell me more than nothing. You've never told me anything.'

'And that's how it's going to be.'

'For always? You mean, when I'm grown up, you're still not going to tell me anything I've a right to know?'

'When you're properly grown up, I may. For now all you need to know is that you haven't got a mum now. You've got me.'

It was difficult after this, to say any more. But Stephen knew that there was a lot more he wanted to know. He said, 'I wish you'd tell me straight out what happened. Did my mum die? Or did she go off somewhere?'

There was a long silence. Then his dad said, 'I'm not going to say any more.'

'It's not fair! You're treating me as if I was a baby! Why do you have to keep secrets like this? Whatever happened to her, I want to know!'

'Can't you trust me to know what's best for you?' his dad asked.

Stephen cried out, 'No! I can't! She was my mum. Everyone else has a mum, why don't I?'

'You'll understand when you're older,' his dad said.

It was the sort of remark that always made Stephen see red. He stood up. 'That's how you always are. "You'll understand when you're older." You've been saying that all my life. I'm sick of being told I'm not old enough to understand. Why don't you try me?' He was standing over his dad now. He wanted to hit him, to take him by the shoulders and shake the answers out of him. He must have looked threatening, because his dad stood up too. He spoke very quietly.

'There's no point in screaming at me and behaving like a spoiled child. I have told you that you haven't got a mother any more. That's enough, Stephen. Please try to

44

control yourself.' After which, his dad walked out of the room.

Stephen stayed where he was. He could have cried with frustration. He was furious with his dad and he was furious with himself. It was true. He had behaved like a child. He might have known that this sort of confrontation was never going to get him anywhere with his dad. He'd seen it before, with other people mostly, that the more someone shouted and raved, the quieter Dad became. It was as if he was saying, though not in words, 'Look at you, losing control like that! You can't make me do anything I don't want to, because I am always master of my feelings. I never give anything away.' Hot angry tears forced themselves out of Stephen's eyes. He wiped them away quickly. His dad must never see him cry. That would only make him even more sure that Stephen was still too young to be trusted with a secret.

9

It was a long time before Stephen had calmed down enough to begin to think in bed that night. He was still too angry to sleep, and he lay on his back, trying to sort out what he knew and what he didn't about his mother.

He couldn't remember her. He had a vague idea that he could recall once being very small, so small that he knew the underside of the kitchen table better than he knew its top, and being coaxed out from behind the same table by a woman. She had called him Deedie, the baby name which he had rejected before he was five years old. She had been tall—but that proved nothing, he was so much smaller that she could have been any height—and she had worn something red. She could have been his mother. But so could she have been any other woman. He was sure she hadn't been his gran, because she never wore skirts that short. It could have been his Aunt Alice, but he didn't think it was. So that was as far as his own memory went, and it didn't help at all.

He tried to think back to his babyhood, but he couldn't remember anything except for a few pictures which didn't hang together and told him nothing. There was a room full of other children. Babies too, and a woman carrying a huge teddy bear, which had somehow frightened him. It was too big. Someone playing a piano very loud and knowing that he was supposed to be joining in a song. A plate of something horrible that he didn't want to eat. He had been sat in front of that plate for what seemed like hours, and then his dad had somehow appeared and rescued him.

After this the pictures became clearer and began to make more sense. There was Gran sitting in a chair. She seemed always to be sitting in a chair, while Aunt Alice moved around and did things. What did she do? Laid the table and poured out tea. Gran drank her tea with long sucking sips. He remembered Gran saying to his dad, 'Who gets your meals?' and his dad saying 'I do. Why should I want anyone coming in and interfering?' He had been impressed by the way his dad had spoken, as if he was angry.

Something he couldn't forget was the first time he'd refused to kiss Gran and Aunt Alice goodbye. Aunt Alice hadn't said anything, but Gran had burst out with, 'Tell him it's his duty to show love for his gran. The only one he's got.' And his dad had said, calmly, like he almost always spoke, 'You can tell him that. I shan't. If he doesn't want to kiss you, he doesn't have to. There wasn't much kissing going on when I was his age.' And they had left without his going through the kissing business, which he'd always hated. Aunt Alice was hairy round the mouth and chin, and Gran smelt. Not exactly horrible, but a stuffy, sweet sort of smell that he didn't like. After that he'd never kissed either of them again. Now, thinking about it, he realized that his dad wasn't any fonder of Gran, even if she was his own mother, than he, Stephen, was.

That must have been when he was seven or eight. So he had known then that there wasn't another gran. He hadn't realized at that age that it was usual to have two grandmothers. He had just accepted that he had only one, and that there wasn't a grandad because Dad's dad had died years ago, when Dad, his son, had been quite a young man. He had been a highly prized printer in a big firm, in the days before everything had been automated. He had wanted Stephen's dad to follow in the same line, but when he'd died and left practically no money, the family couldn't afford the apprenticeship. Stephen's dad had had to take whatever job he could get. Aunt Alice had had a job too, but what she earned wasn't enough for the three of them.

Stephen had asked once, 'What was my grandad like?' and his dad had answered, 'I wish you'd known him.' So Stephen knew that his dad had really liked his father. Perhaps Aunt Alice had liked him too? Poor old thing, she didn't seem to have enough character to like anyone much. She hardly spoke when she was with the others. When she came into a room, she opened the door as little as possible and sort of sidled in, as if she was pretending not to be there at all. Her mother bullied her. It was, 'Alice'll do that,' whenever there was a disagreeable job to be done, but Gran took all the credit. When Stephen and his dad were there for a meal, Gran always claimed that she had provided the food, though they all knew that it was Alice who did the shopping and it was Alice who cooked. Not very well, but at least she tried. Gran didn't do anything but sit in her special chair and criticize. Stephen wondered now if he could get Aunt Alice to talk about his mum. He reckoned probably not, but he could at least have a try.

He fell asleep at last without having come to any conclusion, except that next time he and Dad went to visit his gran, he would see if he could get anything out of Aunt Alice.

He had to wait for nearly a month before he could act on this decision. He and Dad went to visit Gran nearly every other Sunday in the winter, but in the summer their visits depended on all sorts of different things. Dad's job, which sometimes demanded his presence on a Sunday; on the weather, on other engagements. Stephen had long suspected that some of the things Dad thought up for them to do, like driving out to watch a village cricket match, or sitting by a stream with rod and lines (generally not catching anything), or trudging up hills to where Dad thought there'd be a good view, were really excuses not to have to go to visit Gran. He didn't mind; he would rather do almost anything than have to go to spend two hours in that small, stuffy house, where there was nothing to do. No books that he wanted to read, indifferent food, and Gran's conversation, which was all about herself and was loaded with complaints about the neighbours, the Government, the weather, and often about Dad himself. Sometimes he was allowed to watch telly, but on Sunday afternoons there usually wasn't much that interested him.

So it was late June when Stephen and his dad parked in the narrow street outside Gran's house. Looking at it with loathing, Stephen noted the lace curtains drawn closely across the windows, the uncared for front garden, which had no flowers, only laurels with dark spotted leaves hedging the faded front door. He did not want to go inside. And yet he did want to get Aunt Alice to tell him what his dad wouldn't. He dragged his feet as he followed his dad into the narrow hallway and smelt the familiar smell of overcooked vegetables, dust, and old age.

The visit followed the familiar pattern. Exchange of news—only there wasn't any. Enquiries about his progress at school, which he fielded with long-learnt expertise. Enquiries about health, followed by a long recitation of Gran's ailments and accounts of the lack of caring in all the doctors and nurses she had met. Then tea. Occasionally Aunt Alice had not had time to make a cake and had had to buy provisions, and when this happened,

49

tea was the high spot of the afternoon. But not today. Stephen saw with dismay that the usual paste sandwiches, which he loathed, were accompanied by Alice's standard cake. This was called a Victoria sponge, and was hard and dry, with the merest smear of jam in the middle. Stephen ate it. He couldn't afford to hurt Aunt Alice's feelings by refusing a slice. He wanted her to be in a good temper and to like him better than usual.

After tea, feeling mean, he offered to help her wash up, and felt meaner still when he saw her look of pleasure as she accepted. He and Alice carried two trays into the back kitchen and began to unload the remains of the meal.

'I'll wash and you can dry. There's a towel hanging by the door,' she said, running hot water into the bowl in the sink.

For several minutes, Stephen received knives and forks and then cups and saucers from her and dried them in silence. He didn't know how to begin. Then Aunt Alice started talking, asking him questions about what he was doing at school, what games he played, when he would be taking exams. Did he have friends? What were their names? How old were they? He didn't believe she was really interested. He wasn't sure she was even listening to the answers. She kept on saying, 'That's good,' or 'That's nice,' to everything he said. And they were getting to the end of the dishes. In another two minutes they would have finished their work and would have to go back into the living room. He was getting desperate. At last, he cut into a question she was asking about what he was going to do in the holidays, and said, 'Aunt Alice, I want to ask you something.'

He could tell she was surprised by the way she turned right round to face him. Not giving himself time to panic, Stephen said, 'I want to know about my mum.'

50

She turned back to the sink and she went very quiet. He could see her hand shake as she gave a last rub round the washing-up bowl. She didn't answer, but said, as if she hadn't heard him, with forced cheerfulness, 'There! That's all done!'

Stephen said, 'Please! About my mum?'

Again as if he hadn't spoken, she said, 'Thank you so much for helping. You're very kind to your old auntie.'

'Please, Aunt Alice! There isn't anyone I can ask except you.'

She walked over to the door and dried her hands on the roller towel hanging there. She said, 'Let's go back to see Gran and your dad again, shall we?'

Stephen said, 'I don't want to. I want you to tell me what happened to my mum. I've asked Dad and he won't tell me.'

'If your dad doesn't want you to know, you can't expect me to say anything,' she said.

'But he doesn't explain. He hasn't really told me if she's dead or what!'

She looked at him, and he saw terror in her look.

'Is she dead?' Stephen cried out.

'Sh . . . sh . . . sh! They'll hear in there,' his aunt said.

'I don't care.' But he did. His next question came in a lower voice.

'Did she die? When did she die? What happened?' he asked.

'I can't tell you anything. It's your dad should tell you. Not me.' She escaped past him into the passage and opened the living room door. 'Finished washing the dishes. Stephen helped a lot,' he heard her announce in a voice that tried to be normal and bright, but which sounded to him so false that he was surprised that his dad or Gran didn't immediately start up and say, 'What's

51

the matter?' But they didn't and the rest of their visit followed the usual pattern of unmeaning talk about nothing, the early evening news on the telly, then leave-takings, with Gran's reminder that they should come again soon, and his dad's comment once they were outside the front door. 'There! That's it for another few weeks, thank God.'

Stephen wouldn't have been surprised if his dad had asked him if he'd upset his Aunt Alice in any way. But on the way home, Dad seemed no different from usual, and Stephen couldn't summon up the courage to start questioning him again.

But he wanted to. Aunt Alice hadn't told him anything, but what she had said, had suggested that there was something that was being kept from him. Why had she said, 'Your dad should tell you,' if there was nothing to tell?

In bed that night, he went over in his mind all the possible stories there could be about his mum. Perhaps she really was dead. But if so, why didn't they say so? Plenty of kids lost their parents, and though it was sad, it was no disgrace. Perhaps she had killed herself? That would account for the silences, but it still wasn't something to be concealed like a crime. Possibly she had run away with another man. Stephen considered that this was much the most likely of all the possibilities he could think up. It would account for his dad's refusal to speak of her. It would have been a terrible blow to his pride. He would also probably have felt that her going off and leaving him behind would be so hurtful to Stephen that he should not know of it. 'But I'm growing up. They can't not ever tell me. Whatever it is I ought to know,' Stephen said to himself, and turned uneasily on his hot bed. If she's alive, I want to know. I want to see her and find out what really happened, he thought and his busy imagination kept him awake and tormented him until the night cooled down and at last he slept. But even then, he dreamed, and his dreams were uneasy.

10

It was July and hot. Everything seemed to be winding down like the school term, where the pupils were bored and unruly and the teachers were tired and cross.

'Are we going away this holidays?' Stephen asked his dad.

'I haven't made any plans,' his dad said.

'Aren't you due for some time off?'

'I suppose so.'

'Then can't we go somewhere? I'd like to go to the sea.'

'It's late to arrange anything.'

Stephen thought, but didn't quite say, Then why didn't you think of arranging something before now? But he didn't. There was no point in annoying Dad when he was trying to get something out of him.

'Couldn't we go for a bit? We could camp,' he said.

'Camp in what? We haven't got a tent or anything.'

'I could borrow a tent,' Stephen said, not at all sure if he could or couldn't. But he knew that Mike's dad had a tent. He had taken Mike camping in it the summer before last. If Mike's family didn't need their tent this summer, they might lend it to Stephen for a short time.

'Camping's not that simple. You have to find somewhere they let you put the tent up.'

'Have you ever gone camping, Dad?' Stephen asked.

'A long time ago. Rained most of the time.' But his dad laughed as if, in spite of the rain, he might have enjoyed the experience.

'Dad! If I can borrow a tent, can we go?'

'I'll think about it when you've got your tent,' Dad said, and Stephen had the sense not to go on with the subject. He knew how Dad worked.

The next day, he tackled Mike. 'You going away this holidays?' he asked.

'We're going on a package. Spain. Sea'll be warm. I can't wait,' Mike said.

'You going camping there?'

'No, stupid. I said it was a package. We're flying there and it'll be a hotel. This year my mum said, "No more cooking over a camping stove and sleeping on the ground." She wants a proper holiday, where she doesn't have to do all the work. She bullied Himself till he agreed. I can't wait,' Mike said again. Himself was Mike's dad. That was how his mum generally referred to her husband.

Stephen was terribly envious. He'd have loved to fly to Spain and stay in a proper hotel, something he'd never done. But the news was good for him. He said, 'You won't be using your tent, then?'

'I said we're going to a hotel, didn't I? What would we want to take a tent for? On the aeroplane and all,' Mike said.

'Could I borrow it?' Stephen asked.

'The aeroplane? Or the hotel?'

'No, the tent.'

Mike looked serious. 'Dunno. It's my dad's, see? I don't know what he'd say.'

'I'd be careful. Extra careful. Really.'

'You know how to put a tent up?'

'My dad does. He's done it before.'

'You mean you and your dad are going away?'

'We might. If we can have a lend of a tent.'

'Where'd you go?'

'We haven't thought yet. Not far. Because my dad can't take much time off. Somewhere by the sea, I'd like.'

'Your dad's a careful sort of bloke, isn't he? I've seen him. He looks as if he'd be careful.'

'He's careful. He's extra careful,' Stephen said, thinking that this was hardly strong enough for the sort of careful his dad was.

'I'll ask,' Mike said.

'Thanks. Thanks a lot.'

The next day, Mike met him with, 'It's all right. My dad says, you're welcome. And if you come round Sunday, he'll show you how it goes up.'

Stephen reported this at home. 'Mike's dad's going to lend us his tent. And he'll show us how to put it up if we go there on Sunday.'

'I know how to put up a tent,' Stephen's dad said.

'Are they all the same? I mean, if you know how to do one, can you do them all?'

'It's like driving a car. You can work it out, once you know one.'

But he did go with Stephen on Sunday. He said it would be only right. Stephen was anxious. His dad was not a talker and generally found it difficult to get on with people. But Mike's dad was so different, so easy and so friendly, without seeming to notice that his friendliness wasn't immediately returned, that the two dads got on surprisingly well. And Mike's dad was better than his word. He not only lent them his tent, but he added most of the equipment they would need. A ground sheet, two sleeping bags, a camping stove, insect-proof boxes to keep food in, a roof rack, canvas bags for extra clothes.

'It's chilly in the night. You'd better take all the sweaters you've got. And take something to keep the bugs off you while you sleep. First time I went camping, the mosquitoes or something like them made a meal of me.

56

My face swelled right up so that Dolly said she wouldn't have known me.' Dolly was Mike's mum.

'He's all right, isn't he?' Stephen asked his dad as they drove home.

'Talks too much,' his dad replied.

'But it was good he's let us have all this.'

'It's a bit much.'

'But we'll need all the things he's given us. Won't we?'

'We'll see. Anyway, it's lent, not given.'

'I meant lent. So where'll we go, Dad?'

'Have to think. Not too far.'

'The sea?' Stephen prompted.

'We'll see about that.'

Unsatisfactory. But at least he had got past the first step.

The long school term ended. At first it was wonderful enough not to have to get up in the mornings, not to have homework every evening. Then it became less wonderful. Mike was off on his package holiday, Dan was sometimes free, but more often not. He had cousins staying who took up most of his time. Stephen did not know how to fill up the day. He hung around his dad's garage until Ray and Sandy who worked there got fed up with him and told him to go off. Even when he offered to help, they didn't want him there.

He tried cooking, thinking that his dad might be pleased to come home and find a meal ready waiting. But after he had burned one saucepan beyond repair and wasted three eggs and nearly half a pound of butter in a cake that didn't rise in the oven and wouldn't stay together when taken out of its tin, he decided to give up experiments in the kitchen, except for the fry-up which he knew couldn't go wrong. He looked at the garden and meant to have a real go at it and make it as flowery and scented as Mrs Nelson's, where her son-in-law came every weekend and worked for hours at a time. But Stephen got discouraged after half an hour of pulling up weeds. The sweet peas he had sown months ago had come up all right, but for want of watering had not flowered successfully and had produced only a few small, unsatisfactory pods.

He went to the High Street and bought enough milk chocolate to make himself feel uncomfortably sick. He walked round the shop that hired out videos and had computer games and longed for them. But he hadn't got a computer and with Mike away there was no chance of seeing a video or playing any of the games. He almost wished it was term time again.

That Saturday, his dad suddenly said, 'I'm taking a few days off next week. You'd better get packed.'

Unexpected. Stephen said, 'Dad! When are we going?'

'Could go tomorrow if you're ready.'

'I'll be ready.'

'We'll start early. Less traffic.'

'What time?'

'Seven. Got your alarm?'

He had. 'Where'll we go, Dad?'

'Somewhere on the coast. We'll have to look around to find where we're allowed to put the tent.'

'Cornwall? Wales?' He had seen pictures of long beaches and high cliffs.

'Too far. We'll try the south coast.'

He spent that day in a fever of excitement and indecision. Packed the kitbag lent by Mike's father twenty times and twenty times took everything out and re-packed. Couldn't decide what book to take in case there'd be time to read, which pullover would be warmest, whether it should be shorts or long jeans as spares, trainers or flip-flops. Kept on finding he'd left out something he knew he had to have, then filling the bag so full it wouldn't close.

Wondering all the time where they'd be this time tomorrow, what sleeping on the ground would be like, whether it would be proper sea with big waves and an empty beach, whether he'd be able to swim, what the weather would be like. He hoped the beach wouldn't be like some he'd seen on television, so packed with deck chairs and bodies that you couldn't see the sand. Thought, uneasily, how he'd get through whole days spent with Dad alone. If you have a father who doesn't talk except when he has to, you don't count much on him for company.

They got away at a quarter past seven. Not bad, considering that just on the point of leaving, Stephen realized that he'd forgotten to bring his swimming trunks. The front door had to be unlocked for him to go back and find them, which took time, because he hadn't an idea where they were. It was just chance that while he was searching, his eye fell on his jar of keys and he snatched it up, then decided that he was fed up with them. He left the jar by his bed, and ran out to the car. He'd expected Dad to be cross, but nothing was said, and they drove up the street, across town and out into the country.

It seemed a long drive, even though they weren't going to Wales or Cornwall. After the first hour they stopped at a service station and had a sort of breakfast which would do for lunch. Stephen was ravenous and ate sausages and bacon and eggs and mushrooms and fried bread as if he hadn't had a meal for a week. His dad ate less and studied the map, drinking coffee. Presently he said, 'Martelsea.'

Stephen said, 'What?'

'That's where we'll make for. Look! Here on the map.'

Stephen saw the name on the map. In small writing, not a big place, one side of a little headland sticking out

59

into the English Channel. Nothing to mark it out as different from thirty other places on the south coast. He said, 'You been there, Dad?'

'Not for years. It was all right then. Not touristy, undeveloped you might say. We'll try there.'

'How long will it take us from here?'

'About an hour. If you've finished, let's get going.'

It took rather more than an hour to reach Martelsea, and it was another two before they had found a place to pitch the tent. They had driven over heath and wooded lanes which wound up and down hills and finally came out into the town, which was small and old fashioned, two streets running down steeply towards the glittering steel-coloured expanse a little way beyond, which must be the sea. But before reaching that, Stephen's dad insisted they must find the place where they were to spend the night.

They were refused permission to camp more than once before they struck lucky. And it was luck. They had gone into a small shop, half grocery and fruit and veg, half post office, on the edge of the little town, to ask the man behind the counter if he could tell them of anyone locally who might allow them to camp on their land. He was vague and unhelpful and they were just leaving when a woman who had heard the conversation while she was buying stamps, asked Dad who else was with him and how long he wanted to stay. When she heard that it would be for three or four nights, and that he and Stephen made up the whole party, she offered the bit of ground at the end of her garden for their site. She explained that it was rough ground which her nephews had used for playing football when they were younger. She added that there was an outside toilet in her garden which they were welcome to use, and they could come to her door and ask for water if they needed to.

Stephen was anxious. His dad didn't like accepting favours, wasn't easy with anyone, especially strangers. But it was all right. Dad said, 'That's kind of you. Should we pay a sort of rent?' and the woman laughed and said she wouldn't know how much to charge for three nights in a field. She came out of the shop with them and directed Dad to the road that went past her house.

'You can take your things through my garden. You'll see, there's a gap in the hedge. The football pitch's the other side of that,' she said.

The place was perfect. A small area of rough grass, not as big as a real football pitch, separated from the woman's garden and from the road by thick hedges and young trees. Stephen was surprised by the way his dad got the tent rigged up, quick and unfussed, as if he'd been doing it all his life instead of once or twice a long time ago. He could tell from the way his dad went about it, and showed him how to help, that he was in a good temper, which made it easier for Stephen to say, when they'd finished everything, down to unpacking everything they'd need for the night, 'Can we go and look at the sea now?'

'What? Tonight? It'll be getting dark in half an hour.'

'We could go in the car. That'd be quicker.'

'What about eating? We've to eat some time.'

'Couldn't we get fish and chips somewhere in the town? On our way back.'

'We can't stop long at the sea.'

'I don't want to stop long. Just to look at it.'

Dad said, 'Right!' and they went back, through the woman's garden, with pale flowers that smelt more strongly now that it was twilight, into the car, down the hill past shops, mostly shut, towards the sea. Before they reached the shore, Stephen could smell it. It smelt of salt and of hot pebbles and old fish and drying seaweed. He drew long breaths in and wished he could hold them for ever. They drove past tracts of empty land, covered with thistles and long grass and rubbish and came out on to what would, in a prosperous seaside town, have been the front or the esplanade. Here, in this neglected part of the coast, there was a road running parallel to the sea, with a few buildings on the land side; a dilapidated block of flats, a tired looking small hotel, and a row of beach huts. On the sea side there was the sea wall level with the road. The shingle on the shore was piled up almost as high as the wall. The further side of the shingle was the sea.

Now that he was close to it, Stephen saw that what had looked, from a distance, flat and still, was anything but that. It was still grey rather than blue or green, but it was a tumbled grey with moving darker shadows and light points that appeared and disappeared almost before he had caught sight of them. And on the shore below him small waves were curling in over the shingle, coming up, one chasing the wave before it, and then retreating before the next, with a slow rasping sound as the water pulled back between the stones. It was a wonderful noise, and as Stephen's eyes moved across the restless surface to the curved, empty horizon, he knew that it was a wonderful sight. He felt that he could watch the sea for ever.

He looked sideways at his dad and saw that he too was watching the sea. He said, 'It's grand, isn't it?' He wanted to say, 'Thanks for bringing me here,' but he knew that his dad hated any expressions of feeling so he kept quiet.

The light was fading fast. Dad said, 'If we stay here any longer, we'll get caught in the dark,' and turned away towards the car.

Stephen reluctantly turned too, then saw something that made him stop. 'What's that?' he asked, pointing. A small squat tower was placed, incongruously it seemed, right on the edge of the sea wall. It might have been part of a castle wall, but there was no castle near. It looked out of place; even, in the gathering dusk, a little sinister.

'That's the Martello Tower,' Dad said.

'What's a Martello Tower? Why is it there?'

'They built them to prevent the French from landing. Napoleon. You know.'

Stephen did know, vaguely. Napoleon, hundreds of years ago. Before wars were fought with planes and flying bombs. He said, 'Like the Armada?'

They were back in the car now and driving over the empty land between sea and town. Dad said, 'You're only about two hundred years out. But like the Armada because the danger was from the sea. People expected the French troops to land anywhere along here. The Martello towers were built as defences against them. There are several of them, all along the south coast.'

'Can we see some of them? Can I go and look at this one properly tomorrow?'

Dad, as usual, said, 'We'll see.'

But they were driving up one of the little steep streets and Stephen called out, 'Dad! There's a fish and chips! Stop!'

The fish and chips were delicious. They tasted quite different from any others Stephen had had, eaten while sitting on the grass outside the tent, in the light of a hurricane lamp—Mike's dad's, of course. After which, both tired, they decided for bed. Stephen opted to sleep out, promising to come into the tent if it started raining. His dad disappeared under the canvas. Stephen had meant to stay awake to luxuriate in being where he was, to count the stars, to watch the moon rising. But he did none of these things. He was asleep before he had done one of them.

63

11

They spent the morning on the beach, throwing stones at cairns they had built, eating ice creams from a van that came tinkling along the beach road, reading the paper—that was Dad—looking at the sea. That, of course, was Stephen. The sun shone, it was warm. Stephen thought he would try swimming, and did eventually get over painful shingle into water that felt icy at first, but which gradually became bearable, even gentle, and at last was waist deep and he could really swim. It was exhilarating, wonderful. But he was shivering when he came out and his dad made him run on the crunching pebbles for ten minutes. Hard work. He was warm again when he stopped.

He made himself a sort of seat, by pushing the stones around so that he could lean back against them. He began examining them properly. They were all sorts, all colours, all shapes. He found one with a hole right through it and pretended to use it as a spyglass. Very childish, but there was no one to see, and anyway, at the seaside you could be a bit of a child. He collected on his towel the stones he liked best. A small black stone which fitted snugly, as if custom made, into his closed hand. A big black and white stone, with scrawls traced across the white side as if someone was trying to draw something. A very precious amber-coloured stone, almost translucent. An almond shaped stone, so exactly like a sweet that he could have offered it to Dad to suck and taken him in. A smooth brown stone like a bread roll. And there were other treasures. A ball made up of brittle spheres which Dad told him was made of a cuttlefish's egg cases. Half of a broken, long, pale pink and brown razor shell. Clumps of seaweed. Three winkle shells, one badly chipped.

'You'll find other things if you look at the high tide mark,' his dad said, raising his head for a moment from the paper.

So he went up the shifting shingle to the line of seaweed and assorted rubbish that ran just under the sea wall. There were things there he didn't want to find, including several dead birds with oil encrusted feathers. Horrid, he avoided them. There was too much drowned paper, bright orange string, wooden spatulas from ice creams, a canvas sandal, innumerable plastic bottles and bags. He left it, disheartened.

To his surprise, his dad wasn't reading the paper. He was half leaning back, half lying on the shingle, just looking at the sea. Stephen had almost never seen him like this, doing nothing. He sat down beside him and also looked at the sea.

'Like it?' Dad asked.

Stephen couldn't think of any way of expressing how much he liked it, especially to Dad, so he just said, 'Mm.'

'There's a boat going out,' Dad said.

It was a largish boat with a squat funnel and a great deal of white superstructure, pitted with small square panes of glass above the darker main hull.

'Wonder where to,' Stephen said.

'Cross Channel ferry. Going to Dieppe.'

'I wouldn't mind going.'

'If we had longer.'

'It's great here too,' Stephen said. He didn't want to sound as if this holiday wasn't the best he'd ever had.

65

'Time to get something to eat. I wouldn't mind a pub with a garden.'

In the afternoon they went back to the beach. Dad lay back on the stones and went to sleep. Stephen went exploring.

He walked along the front to have a look at what his dad had said was the Martello Tower. It was like a child's idea of a tower, round and stubby and built straight on to the sea wall. You could walk round three quarters of its circle on the road side, the last quarter hung over the shingle on the beach just below. It was made of small bricks cemented together and he could feel, even from outside, how thick and solid the walls must be, so that inside it would be small compared to its outer appearance. It had uneven spaces for windows and at ground level a barred wooden door. Stephen gave it a push, and it creaked, but did not yield. He tried to imagine what it would have been like to be a soldier in there, waiting for Napoleon to come over the sea with an army, to take over England. He would have a gun of some sort, he supposed. Perhaps a sword too. And probably a small cannon, so that he could fire at any ship that looked as if it was a part of the French invading fleet.

It was then that he noticed the change in the weather. The white clouds in the sky were moving faster and sometimes cutting out the sun, there were more white horses out at sea. There was a wind, too, whereas before it had been absolutely calm and hot. He did not hurry back to where his dad was sleeping, but when he got there, Dad was sitting up and looking at the sky, now overcast.

'Hi!' Stephen said, dropping on to the stones beside him.

'Been for a walk?'

'You were asleep.'

'I was awake in the night.'

'You should try sleeping out. It was great.'

'Not tonight, I won't. Weather's changing.'

'There's more wind,' Stephen said. At the same moment, a gust picked up his dad's newspaper, shook it into separate sheets and blew them off over the shingle, up towards the road.

'Catch it!' his dad shouted and he and Stephen raced as fast as they could through the shifting stones. They didn't succeed in getting all the sheets before the last two were blown up to the road and out of sight. They came back to collect the rest of their belongings with what remained of the paper scrunched in their hands.

'It's going to rain,' Dad said.

'No, look. Sun's trying to come out,' Stephen said, as a shaft of sunlight passed swiftly over the shore. It disappeared almost at once, and there was a patter of raindrops on stones and concrete. Then the downpour. They ran for the car.

'You wet?'

'Mm. Dripping.'

'We'll have to dry out somehow back there.'

It is difficult to dry out in a tent when everything outside it is wetter than you are. Stephen was very soon shivering and in a filthy temper. At last his dad said, 'Why don't you go and ask the lady if you can sit in her kitchen for a bit?'

'What for?'

'To get warm. She's got an Aga. I saw it.'

'What's an Aga?'

'Sort of stove. Stays on all the time. It'd be warm.'

Stephen baulked. 'I don't like to.'

'She said we could ask.'

'She said for water. That isn't water.'

'It's because of rain. That's water, isn't it?' One of his dad's rare jokes.

'But . . . it'd mean staying there.'

'Not for long, it wouldn't.'

Stephen didn't want to. He thought he could count on his dad's dislike of strangers and of asking favours. He was surprised when dad walked out of the tent in his anorak and came back a minute later with the lady under an umbrella. She called to him through the tent flap door. 'You in there! You're to come into the house to get dry. And bring your wet things.'

Dad was there, collecting his soaking shirt and trousers for him. 'Go on!'

'Aren't you coming?'

'I'm not as wet as you. You can take my trousers, though. She says she'll hang the things up near the Aga and they'll be dry by morning.'

So Stephen found himself conducted under a vast striped umbrella up to the kitchen door, where the dripping garments were taken from him and hung on a curious contraption that hung from the ceiling near the compact bulk of the Aga stove. He had to admit it was good to sit in a warm dry place to feel his feet gradually thawing out. The lady sat at the kitchen table, opposite to him. She was shelling peas into a white pudding basin. Besides vegetables, the table was also covered with papers. A newspaper, a writing block, and a pile of opened letters.

'How did you manage to get so wet?' she asked.

'We were on the beach. It was sunny at first. Then the wind started blowing and all of sudden there was the rain.'

'It can take you by surprise.'

'I didn't think it could change so suddenly.'

'The wind can get up in minutes. There's going to be a proper storm tonight.'

'Will there be big waves?'

'Over the road. Probably.'

He watched her. She was quite old. Sixty at least, he thought. She had grey hair pulled back from a bony face and fastened at the back of her neck in an untidy sort of knot. She was wearing a man's check shirt in red and orange colours and denim jeans. He decided that he liked her looks. He didn't like ladies who dressed up too much. He said, 'Shall I help you with the peas?'

She said, 'Thank you, but they're almost done.'

He felt awkward just sitting there, doing nothing, but he didn't want to leave this comfort. 'Anything you'd like me to do?'

'Can you peel potatoes?'

'Easy. Only I don't like peelers. I'm better with a knife.'

She said, 'So am I.' She put before him three large potatoes and a knife. It was beautifully sharp. 'When you've done them, would you put them in this bowl?' She pushed a pudding basin half full of water across the table. She was now slicing onions, very fast.

'What's the water for?'

'To prevent them going the wrong colour. It's water with lemon in it.'

There was a question he wanted to ask, but he felt awkward about it. He kept on putting it off, so that at last it came out too fast and sounded almost angry. Not at all what he felt. He said, 'I don't know your name.'

'It's Oddie. I'm Miss Oddie. It used to be quite a common name around here. Now I think I'm almost the only one. I don't know your name, either.'

'I'm Stephen.'

'That's a nice name. I've known several Stephens and I've liked them all.'

He was embarrassed. 'I've done the potatoes.'

69

'That's fine. Thank you very much.'

'You're welcome.'

She left the table and put a pan of water on the Aga.

'Who cooks most when you're at home?' she asked.

'Dad mostly. I'm not much good except for fry-ups.'

He dreaded the question which was sure to come next. 'Is your mother a good cook?' When she asked it, what was he going to answer? But to his immense relief and surprise she didn't ask it. Instead, she came back to the table and began to clear it of pea husks and potato peelings. Then she began to sort the pile of letters.

'I'd better be getting back,' Stephen said. He didn't want to outstay his welcome.

'Not unless you want to. Wait until you're warm all through. Would you like a hot drink? Tea?'

'Tea'd be great. Thanks,' Stephen said.

She made the tea in a small china teapot, ribbed and rounded, with a delicate pink and white pattern. The prettiest he'd ever seen. It matched the cup and saucer she put in front of him. He wondered if she treated all her visitors so grandly. He'd never had a whole pot of tea just for himself. There was also a milk jug and a sugar basin full of white lumps. The biscuits came out of a tin like a red pillarbox.

'Aren't you having any tea?' he asked.

'I had mine an hour ago. But thank you for asking.'

While he ate and drank, she continued to sort the letters. Presently she looked up and asked, 'Do you collect stamps?'

He said, 'No.'

'Pity. I get some quite interesting foreign ones.'

There seemed no answer to this.

'Do you collect anything? Badges? Memorabilia?'

'I don't know what that is.'

'I'm not sure that I do, either. Things, I think. Things that remind you of something. Anything.'

'Doesn't sound very interesting.'

'I don't think it is. Not very. Often just a lot of clutter.'

Without knowing he was going to, he heard himself say, 'I do collect keys.'

'Keys? Do you? What sort of keys?'

He wished now he'd held his tongue. 'I don't know. Any sort.'

'Old keys? How many have you got?'

'Not many. Some of them are old.'

'And how do you find them? Do you buy them?'

'I haven't yet. The ones I've got, I just found in the garden.'

'And have you tried them on doors? Have you found any that fit?'

'Not that many,' Stephen said, embarrassed. He certainly wasn't going to tell her about the keys that did fit.

'I think that's very interesting. I've never known anyone who collected keys. I tell you what . . . '

She got up suddenly and went to the door. 'Stay there a minute. I might have something to add to your collection.'

Stephen stayed. He wished he hadn't blurted out that about his keys. But he had a feeling that this lady wasn't the sort to go on asking questions which she saw could be awkward. Just as she hadn't asked anything about his mother. In another minute she was back in the kitchen with something in her hand. She laid it on the table in front of him.

'Will you have this?' she said.

It was not a very big key, but it was immensely solid. Stephen picked it up and felt its weight. As he held it in his hand, he had the ridiculous idea that it had character, as if it had been a person. Comparing it with his other keys, he thought that Yale keys were business-like, no-nonsense keys, practical. You could be sure that each one would do its proper job and nothing else. There were boys he knew at school like that, who were sensible, didn't forget to take notes from their parents to school or from the school to their parents, didn't lose their possessions, did their homework, knew the right answers in class. The big key with the squiggly top was a romantic key that could have belonged to a long-ago castle, shouldn't really have opened the door of that sham house that had no inside. This key was different from any of the others. It was short and stubby and rounded and friendly. If it had been a person it would have been someone Stephen would have liked. He saw at once that it should belong to a friendly building.

He was ashamed of himself. How could he be so childish?

All this thinking had taken no time at all. He said, 'Are you sure? You don't want to keep it?'

'I don't want to keep it. It doesn't open any lock that I've got. I'd be proud to donate it to your collection.'

He said, 'Thanks a lot. It's great.' He had run out of words.

'If your collection ever becomes famous, you could label that one, "From Martelsea".'

'I'll put your name. Only it won't ever. Be famous, I mean.'

'You never know.'

He said, 'I ought to be going.'

'Are you warm right through? You sure?'

'Sure.'

She got up to see him to the door. 'Nothing you want for the evening?'

'I don't think so. Thanks.'

'Look, it's stopped raining.' It had. The sun was shining between huge white clouds. Raindrops glittered on the leaves of the garden plants.

'You'll be able to sit out for your supper,' she said.

Stephen said, 'Bye! And thanks a lot. The key's great.'

'It was a pleasure,' she said.

Sitting on the ground sheets and eating delicious half burned sausages and baked beans heated up over the little stove, Stephen said, 'Good day, Dad.'

'Glad you enjoyed it.'

'I wish we weren't going back so soon.'

'There's another day.'

'I know. But I'd like to stay for a long time. A week.'

'I can't take that much time off. Anyway, I miss my bed.'

Finding the ground hard that night, Stephen was inclined to agree.

12

The next morning the rain had stopped. Torn clouds raced across the sky, and there was a wind that blew the nearby trees into feather duster shapes. It was much colder.

'What'll we do today?' Stephen asked.

'We could go into Brighton. You should see the Pavilion.'

'Could we go this afternoon?'

'What about this morning?'

'I'd like to go back to the beach.'

'Too cold to sit about. Or swim.'

'I just want to see it again. We don't have to sit.'

They walked to the beach. Each step that got them nearer to the sea was made more difficult by the wind. When they actually reached the front, it was quite difficult to stand still. The wind hurled itself at them, buffeted them, snatched at their jackets, tore at their hair. The sea was huge. Great waves tumbled over the shingle, threw spray and small pebbles up over the road. The stones crashed. Stephen could feel the sea wall shake with the power of the ocean.

'Bedlam,' his dad said.

'It's exciting,' Stephen said.

'May be exciting, but it's bloody cold. Better go back.'

'You go. I want to stay for a bit.'

'What for?'

'I like looking at the waves.'

'You'll get soaked. It's going to rain again.'

'If it does, I'll shelter.'

'You'll stay on the wall?'

Stephen shouted 'YES.' Then felt bad at shouting. But you had to shout to make yourself heard above the wind.

His dad said, 'All right. Don't stay too long. Got your watch?'

'Mm. It's half ten.'

'Be back there by half eleven, then.'

Stephen nodded and saw his dad walk down the slope away from the screaming wind, relieved, no doubt, to leave it behind. Now that he was alone, Stephen knew what he was going to do. He struggled along the wall to the Martello tower. Lucky that there was no one near enough to see what he was doing. As he went, he looked at the tremendous grey waves with white crests that came hurtling towards the shore. He almost enjoyed the shiver with which the land greeted these waves. He supposed that it was used to it. The same sort of waves must have been chasing each other in to pound the solid ground, to threaten it like this, for years. What he was seeing was like seeing history, because it couldn't have been much different a hundred, a thousand, a million years ago. When the squat stone tower had been built and the people here were afraid that Napoleon was going to land, the sea would have looked and behaved just the same. Had they ever mistaken the crash and the shaking of the waves for gunfire? Had they ever looked fearfully out of their houses to see if the tumult was the beginning of war, and been relieved to find that it was only the sea in a rage? Something they'd experienced before and would again?

He had reached the tower. When he was on the land side, sheltered from the wind, it was quiet compared to the racket he'd come out of. He walked round—and into the wind again—until he reached the door. Then he pulled Miss Oddie's key out of his pocket and put it into the

75

ragged keyhole. He had been sure it would fit, and it did. It took a little strength to turn it, and it grated. No one had turned a key in that door for a long time. The door creaked on its hinges, too, as he pushed it open and walked in.

13

He had expected the interior of the tower to be darker than it was. There was a little, a very little light coming in from somewhere above his head. There was just enough light for him to be able to see that he was not alone.

Someone else was there, standing still and observing him. His heart gave a loud thump. He couldn't see what the moving thing was. He wondered, horribly, if it could be a wild animal which had been shut up here for ages. But it didn't move like a hungry animal. It now came quite close to him and he saw, with immense relief, that it was a boy. Quite a small boy, a lot smaller and younger than he himself was.

The boy said, 'I got here first.'

'All right,' Stephen said, not quite knowing what the boy meant.

'Did any of the others see you come in here?' the boy asked.

'What others?' Stephen asked.

'The others who're hiding like us.'

'I'm not hiding,' Stephen said.

'If you're not hiding, why did you come in here?'

Stephen did not understand this. He did not want to try to explain why he had come into the tower, so he said, 'How did you get in? Have you got a key too?'

'You don't need a key to get in here. It's never locked,' the boy said.

'You mean it's just left open all the time?'

'Of course. Why would anyone want to lock up an old cellar?' the boy said.

'It isn't a cellar. It's a Martello tower,' Stephen said.

The boy said, 'A *what*?'

'A Martello tower.'

'Why do you call it that? You know it's really Mrs Robinson's cellar.'

'Who's Mrs Robinson?' Stephen asked.

'You know. Marjorie and Stella's mum. It's her house.'

Stephen was completely confused. The tower couldn't be anyone's house. Could it? He said, 'I don't know what you're talking about.'

'You know Marjorie and Stella. They're at your school in . . . ' He said some name Stephen had never heard before.

'Here, where do you think we are?' Stephen asked. He began to wonder if this boy was crazy.

'We're in Mrs Robinson's house, of course. You're teasing, Deedie, aren't you?' the boy said.

Stephen experienced again that whirling feeling in his head that he'd had before in the garden, when the woman in the garden had said this name. She had claimed that she had known him since he was a baby, and now here was this boy making the same mistake. And now he saw who the boy was. He was Chris, the child who had been cutting his birthday cake. He said, 'I'm not Deedie and I don't know you. And we're not in anyone's cellar, we're in the Martello tower in Martelsea.'

He was so positive that the boy seemed shaken. He said, 'I wish you wouldn't tease. How could it be a tower in Mrs Robinson's house? Anyway, I know it's her cellar, because I came down the steps to it when I wanted to hide.'

'Where's Mrs Robinson's house?' Stephen asked.

'Hunnicut Road, Sydney. Round the corner from us,' the boy said.

78

Stephen said, 'Sydney!' He said, 'You mean, Sydney, Australia?' and the boy said, 'Yes. Australia. Where did you think it was?'

'You're crazy,' Stephen said, not quite certain whether it was the boy or he himself who was crazy. He said, 'Here, I'll show you. If I open the door you can see where we are. We're not in anyone's house, we're right on the edge of the sea wall.'

The key was still in his hand. He approached the door and opened it. To his relief, he saw the sea wall stretching away from him, with the grey water beyond. He turned to say to the boy, 'There! You see?' But behind him the tower was dark and empty. His voice echoed back from the bare walls. He felt he could not bear to go inside again. He banged the heavy door behind him and walked back to Miss Oddie's garden.

14

Stephen was pleased to spend the afternoon with Dad in Brighton in a perfectly ordinary sort of way. He loved the outside of the Pavilion. It was an Arabian Nights sort of building, and didn't seem to have much to do with the rest of the town. He wasn't particularly interested in the interior of the building, though his dad seemed to enjoy looking at exhibitions of costumes and china and at the vast dinner table set for about a hundred guests. They bought ice lollies and ate them as they walked out on the long pier. Stephen looked sideways at Dad and thought he looked funny as he licked his lolly. Almost human, Stephen said to himself, and then felt guilty. Dad had been all right these three days, not as critical as usual. But he was still difficult to get close to. No, not difficult. Impossible.

They sat at the end of the pier. The sea had quieted down since the day before. There were still some little white crested waves coming in, but when they reached the beach they were harmless.

The next morning, they took down the tent, packed the car, and said goodbye to Miss Oddie. 'It's been fine. Kind of you to let us park in your field,' Dad said, with his usual difficulty in putting what he felt into words.

'My pleasure. You were no trouble. And I was glad to have the opportunity to meet you,' she said.

Stephen was really sorry to be leaving. He liked Miss Oddie. He wouldn't mind seeing her again some time. He said, 'Thanks for everything. For having us here, I mean. And for the water. And the key.'

'You were very welcome. Perhaps you'll come back some time?'

'I will if I can,' Stephen said. Then they went out to the car and Dad drove away.

'What was that about a key?' he asked.

'Just she gave me a key.'

'Key for what?'

'A sort of collection I've got.'

'Does this key of hers open something?'

He said, 'I'm not sure.' He couldn't possibly tell Dad that it had opened the door of the Martello tower.

'Not much use then, is it?'

Stephen did not answer this. He was grateful that his dad did not ask any more questions about the key.

He was sorry when they arrived back home. After the stony beach and the tall chalk cliffs and especially after the sea, their street looked dull. He wondered how he was going to employ himself for the rest of the holidays. He wished he could have stayed on in Miss Oddie's field. Perhaps he could have found work in the town. She might even have employed him herself, though he didn't know what for. He wished he had thought of asking her.

Mike was still away. But Dan had not yet gone. Stephen went round to see him and was cheered by a plan to go off for the day on their bikes to a river some miles off where there might be fish.

A day or two after they'd been to the river (and failed to find any fish but had met a great many mosquitoes), he was standing outside the shop that sold videos and computer games, when someone behind him said, 'Hi!' It was Alex, eating an ice lolly. He hadn't seen her approaching and was not pleased. He felt the same embarrassment he'd felt before. But she seemed perfectly friendly. She said, 'Haven't seen you for ages. You been away?'

Stephen said, 'Yes, for a bit. Not long.'

'So've we. We went to Wales for a week. To the sea. It was lovely. Where did you go?'

'We went to the sea, too.' He didn't want to go on with this conversation.

'Did you swim? I did. It was ever so cold.'

'Yes, I did.'

'That's why we haven't been around. Well, we did come here about a month ago, and I called into your garden, but no one answered.'

Stephen didn't answer this.

'Wait a tick,' she said, and went off. Stephen was relieved. Perhaps she'd got the message that he didn't want her around. But two minutes later she was back, with a second ice lolly.

'Here. You look as hot as I am.'

He hadn't meant to take it, but it was in his hand. Then it seemed stupid not to eat it. And he was much too hot.

'Thanks.'

'You're welcome. Let's sit on this bench,' she said.

They licked their lollies. Stephen was angry with himself. He couldn't get up and leave now.

'We're staying here this week. My mum's tidying up Uncle Joe's house for him.'

There didn't seem to be anything to answer to that.

'That day. Why were you so cross with me? I hadn't done anything to you, had I?' Alex asked suddenly. So she hadn't forgotten.

'No.' He couldn't tell her that he'd thought she was a boy.

'What was it then? You were upset by that house, weren't you? Something happened in there that you didn't like.'

He couldn't explain. She would certainly think he was mad. She was going on, 'That's when you asked me about people having doubles.'

He said, 'That was because I'd met some people who thought they knew me, and I don't know them.'

'Perhaps you look like someone they knew long ago. Before you can remember.'

No. It was more peculiar than that. These people seemed to think they knew him now.

'Did you see them inside that house?'

'One of them I did.'

'You've seen some more of them somewhere else?'

He said, reluctantly, 'Yes.'

'Not in that house?'

'No. In a garden.'

'And they thought you were someone else too? Then you must have a double. It's funny no one else has noticed it. What are these people like?'

'Ordinary. Except . . . '

'Except what?'

'Their voices. They've got some sort of weird accent. I don't know what it is.'

'You mean they're foreigners?'

'Not exactly. They talk English like we do. It's just an accent. And some of the words they use aren't like ours.'

'Like what?'

'They told me not to be so goofy.'

'They say that in Australia,' Alex said.

'How'd you know?'

'Heard it on the telly.'

Australia! The boy in the Tower had said, 'Sydney, Australia.'

'Are you sure you don't know them? Never did?'

'Quite sure.'

'But they live over here? Perhaps it's just in Australia you've got a double. Are they over here for a visit, then?'

Stephen said gloomily, 'I don't know. None of it seems to make sense.'

Alex said, 'Where do you meet these people? The first was in the funny flat house, wasn't it?'

'That's right.'

'Where else?'

'I told you. In a garden. In St Edmund's Square.'

'In the square! Are they very posh, then?'

'No. Why?'

'Because it's only posh people with a lot of money live in the square.'

'Well, they aren't posh at all. I don't know how they got there, anyway.' He remembered the young woman from next door saying that the house hadn't been occupied for months. So those people must have been trespassers, just like him.

'Anywhere else?'

It seemed ridiculous, but having started to tell her, he had to go on. 'While we were away.'

'What, by the sea?'

'In a sort of tower.'

'They were in a tower?'

'One of them was. A boy. Quite small.'

'What was he doing in a tower?'

'Hiding. He said it was a game.'

'And he knew you too?'

'Said he did. But . . . '

'What?'

'He thought we were in Australia. He must have been crazy.'

Alex said, 'Wait a minute. You said those other people had funny accents. Were they Australian?'

'Could have been. Yes.' Now that she'd said it, he knew she was right.

'So they're somewhere around over here?'

'That last one was in Martelsea. Where my dad and I'd gone on holiday.'

'Seems like they're everywhere,' Alex said.

'That's how I feel.'

'You don't like them?' she asked.

'It's not that. It's that I don't like them knowing everything about me and I don't know them.'

'Do they know everything about you?'

He didn't want to tell her that what they did know was his baby name. 'They think they do.'

She was thinking hard. 'Is there anything special about the places you meet them at? Or is it just anywhere?'

Inside the flat house. In the Square garden. Inside the Martello tower. He said, 'No. Just seems to be anywhere.' Then, remembering, he said, 'It's like as if I always have to go through a door. Then they're there.'

'You mean they're always the other side of the door?'

'It's like that. Yes.'

'Suppose the doors let you in to a different sort of life?'

'You mean Sci-Fi sort of stuff?' He wanted immediately to get rid of the idea.

'Something like that. Only . . . ' She stopped, mid-sentence.

'Go on.'

'You'll say it's stupid.'

'Never mind. Just say what you were going to.'

She said, suddenly, in quite a different tone, 'Do you ever play the ''If'' game?'

'What's that?'

She said, 'It's sort of wondering what you'd be doing if something different had happened. Like ''What would

85

you do if you were on a plane and there was a hijacker?'' or ''What would you do if you won the lottery?'' or ''Who would you be if you could choose to be anybody?'''

Stephen recognized it at once. 'I don't play it with anyone. It's the sort of thing my dad doesn't like.'

'Mine doesn't either. But my mum and I play it a lot. I told you, when we were talking about Sherlock Holmes. It's a game my mum and I play.'

'What's that got to do with Australia and these people?'

'I just wondered. Suppose there's another life going on somewhere where you might have been if something different had happened?'

'I don't understand.'

'I mean, suppose a long time ago you did something that sort of pinned you down to being here like this. Being you. And if it had happened differently, you might be in Australia with those people. And they think you are really there. It's sort of another you.'

'You mean there are two of me?'

'In a way, I suppose so. Only this here is more real, so you don't know about the other life except when you go through one of those doors. Then you find out you're there. But of course you wouldn't know anything about it because most of the time you're here.'

'Sounds crazy.'

'I knew you'd say that,' she said.

He found that he did not want to hurt her feelings. 'I don't mean you're crazy. Only I don't see how it would work.'

'I don't either. Only I've always wondered if it couldn't. My dad . . . ' She stopped.

'Your dad what?'

'He could have been in the team. Playing football.'

'Which team?' Stephen asked.

She told him and he gasped. 'He must have been really good.'

'He was. Only he had an accident to his knee. They did an operation and they said he could go back and play again, but if he got hurt again, that'd be it. It'd be much more serious. So he had to decide what to do.'

'Didn't he go on playing?'

'No. He said it wasn't worth the risk.'

'Not to play in that team? He must be crazy!' Stephen said, hardly able to believe that it wouldn't have been worth any risk.

'No, he isn't! You've no right to say that! You don't know anything about it,' Alex said, flaring up.

'I know about football,' Stephen said.

'But you don't know my dad.'

Stephen nearly said, 'And I don't want to.' To know a man who could have been one of those heroes and who had turned down the chance just because of a little accident to his knee? He said, 'You don't understand about football.'

'How d'you know I don't?'

'Because you're a girl.'

'That's all you know. Girls can know about football just as well as boys. They can play it too.'

'Not generally, they don't.'

They stared at each other, both furious. Then suddenly, Stephen felt bad. He had no right to criticize her dad, whom he didn't even know. He wouldn't have liked it if she'd started telling him where his own dad was wrong. He said, 'It must have been hard for him.'

'Yes, it was.' She was still angry.

'He might have been famous! He'd have made thousands of pounds! Millions, probably.'

'That's what my mum and I play the ''If'' game about. We say, ''Where would we be now if Dad had gone on playing?'' '

87

'Where d'you think you'd be?'

'No idea. We'd have a lot more money than we do now, that's for sure.'

'Don't you wish he hadn't decided not to?'

'I'm not sure. I suppose we'd have been famous too. My mum says she wouldn't have liked that.'

'She'd have liked being rich, wouldn't she?'

'Suppose so. Anyway, I only told you so you'd see what I meant. Sometimes I imagine there's another one of me living in a huge house with lots of money, and Dad being famous. That's why I thought perhaps there's really another one of you living somewhere.'

'In Australia, you mean?'

'I suppose it could be. Do you think your dad ever thought of going out there?'

'I shouldn't think so.' But something Dad had said, months ago, sounded in Stephen's mind. He'd said something about the other side of the world. Who was it he'd said it about? Not himself. Stephen couldn't for the moment remember, and Alex was asking him something.

'How do you get through the doors?'

'I've got some keys,' he said.

'Like that big one you opened the door with in the end house you said was too thin to be real?'

'That's right. I found one when I was digging in the garden.' He remembered that that was the day he'd first talked to Alex through the shrubs.

'Did you find the others too?'

'Mm. I was going to have a sort of collection. And one I was given.'

'I wonder if they'd work for me? Perhaps I'd find I was in America and Dad was a millionaire.'

Somehow he was sure his keys wouldn't work for her.

She stood up. 'I've got to go now. If you get to that place again, please tell me.'

88

'I might.' But he didn't mean to.

'I'd really like to know about it.'

'How long are you staying here? I mean, with your mum's uncle?'

'Three more days. Bye. Be seeing you.' Then she was gone.

15

Stephen went home. Dad hadn't got back from work yet, so he had the flat to himself, which was good. He felt as if he had more thinking to do than he'd ever had in his life.

Suppose Alex was right? He had not wanted to believe her when she'd explained her idea about the 'If' game really working, but now that he thought about it again, it did seem possible. Not likely, but just possible. Then that would mean that when he was the other side of one of those doors, he was in Australia, living the other life that he would have lived all the time—If.

That was the question. If—what? He must find out whether Dad had ever thought of emigrating. And now he remembered what Dad had said about 'the other side of the world'. It wasn't about himself. It was about Stephen's mum's family. They were the other side of the world. That could be Australia, probably was. That made a sort of crazy sense. He, Stephen, might be living with them instead of with Dad in England. He wondered why they had gone there. He wondered if his mum had gone with them. That might explain why his dad wouldn't talk about her. If she'd chosen to go and leave him, he wasn't likely to be thinking of her with much affection. He'd be angry and hurt.

Stephen knew that he had got to find out about his mum. Whatever had happened, he ought to know. If she was really dead, he wanted to know that too. He had to find out why his dad wouldn't talk about her. That was the problem. With any ordinary dad, Stephen thought, he could have asked and been told the truth. But his dad was a clam. He couldn't be made to talk. And Stephen's attempt with Aunt Alice had failed. He wondered if there was anyone else who knew the truth and who would be willing to tell him.

Suppose Alex was right? Suppose that when he went through one of those special doors, he really did find himself living another life which had somehow got by-passed in favour of this one here? The people there must be his mum's family. All he had to do was to get back there and ask.

He was surprised to discover how much he didn't want to. There had been something disagreeable about the occasions on which he'd met those people—a feeling that they wanted to claim more from him than he wanted to give. They assumed that he belonged to them. But he did not belong, either to them or to the places where he saw them. It was like finding that he was wearing the wrong clothes, or even that he had the wrong kind of skin. He wanted to stay where he was, in the life he knew and understood, not to get involved in that other life, with people he felt were strangers.

He did not have to. And even if he wanted to, he was not sure how to set about it. He would have, he supposed, to go through a door. But which door? He supposed that when he saw it, he would know. He had had the same extraordinary feelings about all three doors he'd been through before. But then he hadn't been unwilling to go through them, he had, in fact, wanted to. Now he didn't. He almost dreaded finding another door.

For a long time he didn't find it. The autumn term had begun, the pavements were covered with wet brown leaves, and the weather was getting colder. He was in a new class at school with a new teacher, whom he didn't like as much as Mr Selsdon who had taught him before. Most of his friends had moved up with him, and life seemed to be much the same as it had always been. He began to forget. Or rather, he never completely forgot, but he was able to think about other things for quite long periods at a time. Except that when he was outside the house and the school, his eyes were constantly alert for the door which he would know he had to go through. It was half annoying, half exciting. He told himself often that it was all stupid. Alex's explanation of what had happened in the summer couldn't be true. Anyone could play the 'If' game, but it was only a game. It wasn't scientifically possible to find yourself in a quite different place, living another life by just walking through a door. He didn't believe it. And yet he was jumpy. And in a quite contradictory way, he was carrying the long dark key from the garden with him whenever he left the house.

When he did see the door, he didn't at first recognize it. It was the October half term holiday, a whole week with nothing particular to do. Dad was working, of course. Stephen decided that he would make a map of his part of the town, a proper map, drawn to scale, and with all the small alleyways and passages that ordinary maps left out. Because the terrain was hilly, and the town had grown out of a village, there were a lot of foot passages and secret byways which Stephen would have liked to believe were known to very few people besides himself. He went out, one cool, sunny morning, armed with pencil and paper, a spring measure, and a ball of string which he thought might help with the measuring.

It was frustrating work. Adding up the measurements, which he was having to do all the time, was difficult, and he had a disagreeable idea that his addition was often wrong. He wished he had someone to help. But both Dan and Mick had been scornful of the whole idea. He didn't want to ask either of them. Alex would have done as he asked, but he didn't think she was staying with Mr Jenkins this week. However, he didn't mean to give up until he had plotted at least one small area. Several people stopped to ask what he was doing. Some of them gave him advice, most of which was impossible to follow, since he hadn't got the right equipment. But in spite of finding it difficult and tiring, he was quite enjoying exploring the bits of the town that he'd never seen before. He was standing in one of the small side roads, bordered with little mean houses, their front windows right on the street, when he suddenly shivered. His spine felt chilled and his heart had given a sort of hop and then beat much faster than usual. For a moment he was giddy. He put out a hand to steady himself, and found that he was leaning against a door.

It wasn't quite like any of the other doors in the street. They were all front doors, up a couple of steps, to the little houses. This was a door that must lead into a covered passage between two houses, since it had no steps, and there was no muslin-curtained window next to it. Stephen looked at it for a long time. He knew that this was the door he had meant to be looking for, but now that he had found it, he did not want to go inside. But he had to know what had happened to his mum. And this might be a way of finding out. So, after a minute or two, during which he stood uncertainly in the street, he pulled the long dark key from his pocket and tried it in the keyhole of the door.

He half hoped it wouldn't turn. But it did, smoothly. He pushed the door open and stepped, to his astonishment, not into a narrow covered passage, but into the glare of hot sun. There was concrete under his feet and he was looking at a park, leafy with luxuriant trees and shrubs. Directly in front of him were two tennis courts. On the nearest were four women playing a doubles match.

He stood and watched them. Not one of them was very good. Their serves were half-hearted and seldom went into the right part of the court. But they seemed cheerful, calling out encouragement to their partners and the score in loud voices, in what he was sure were Australian accents. Quite soon the game came to an end, and they all left the court, mopping red, perspiring faces and gathering together at a bench at the side of the court where they had left a pile of garments. One of them saw Stephen and called out to him. 'Hi! Deedie! Come for a game?'

Stephen had never played tennis. It was not one of the sports on offer at his school. He shook his head.

'Wally'll be here soon. He'd take you on,' one of the women said.

Stephen said, 'No, thanks. It's too hot.' And who was Wally?

'You're right, there. I didn't mean to play, but Rose persuaded me,' the eldest and hottest of the four said. She nodded her head at the woman opposite to her. Stephen presumed that this was Rose. He looked at her with interest.

'If it's like this this early in the summer, what I say is, what's it going to be at Christmas?' Rose said.

Summer? Then he was on the other side of the world. October was the beginning of the Australian summer, Stephen knew. He had got himself to the right place, but he couldn't see how he was going to get the information he wanted. You can't suddenly address four overheated ladies, who think you have come out for a game of tennis, to ask them questions about someone who may or may not belong to their family and who may or may not have been your mother.

He decided that Rose would be the easiest one to question. She was the youngest, and because he'd heard her name before, at least he'd know how to address her.

He waited until all four had collected their various clothes and belongings, and begun to stroll along flower-bordered paths towards a low brick building, which was presumably the club house. Stephen was wondering how on earth he could detach Rose from the others, but luck was on his side. When they reached the building, and the oldest woman said, 'What about tea?' Two of the others agreed that tea would be just what they needed, but Rose said, 'I won't, thanks all the same. If I'm not home when Chris gets back, he'll never get down to his homework.'

She turned to leave the others, sitting at a table on the veranda, and Stephen found it natural to fall into step beside her, having also refused tea on the grounds that he wasn't thirsty.

'You coming with me? That's nice,' she said.

'I'll see you home,' Stephen said, hoping that her home wasn't too far away.

'I've got the car here,' she said, and Stephen saw that they were entering the car park. She opened the door of a small red car and motioned to him to get into the passenger seat.

'Sure it's all right, my coming with you?' Stephen asked.

'Chris'll be pleased. He thinks you're the tiger's whiskers,' she said. Stephen was sure that she was Chris's mum. So where did his own mum fit into this family? He had no idea who the other three tennis players might be.

She drove competently through heavy traffic. Stephen waited until they had turned into a complex of smaller roads. Then he said, 'Rose!'

He saw that she did not like this. She said, 'You cheeky digger! It's Aunt Rose to you, and don't you forget it.'

He said, 'How come you're my aunt?'

'What do you mean, "How come?" I've always been your aunt, haven't I?'

'Because you're my mum's sister?' It was a guess, and he felt brave.

Again he could see that she was disturbed. She said, 'Let's just say I'm your proper aunt and leave it at that.'

'But were you my mum's sister?'

'What about it, if I was?'

'I wanted to ask you. About my mum.'

She looked at him quickly. Then she said, in a very quiet voice, 'We don't talk about her.'

'Why not?'

She said, 'Wait till we get indoors, will you? I can't park the car while I'm thinking what to tell you.'

She drove into the parking space in front of a small house. They both got out of the car. Rose locked it, then she opened the front door and called, 'Chris! Chris! I'm back!' A voice from somewhere inside called, 'All right! In the kitchen.'

It was a large, well fitted kitchen. It seemed to have all the kitchen machinery Stephen had ever heard of. Chris, the boy he had last seen in the Martello tower—or should he say in Mrs Robinson's cellar?—was sitting at the table, eating. His mother said, 'Look who I've brought home with me!' and the boy said, 'Good-o,' and went on eating.

'Sit down. I'll get you some Coke,' Rose said. From an enormous refrigerator, she took two cans of Coke, pushed one across to Stephen and opened the other for herself. She looked at Stephen, and then at Chris. It was clear that she was telling him that she wouldn't talk in front of the boy.

'What sort of a day at school?' she asked and Chris said, 'Lousy. I couldn't do the maths and Peter made me stay in and go over them again with him when the others were outside.'

'Bad luck,' Rose said. Her voice was absent. She wasn't really thinking about Chris and his maths.

'Are you any good at maths?' Chris asked Stephen and Stephen said, 'No. Not very. I'm always being kept in to do things again.'

'You see? It's in the genes!' Chris said to his mother.

'Don't you start talking about genes. You don't pay attention in class, that's why you can't do your sums,' his mother said.

Stephen felt that this could go on for longer than he could bear. He said to Rose, 'Aunt Rose, I wanted to ask you a question.'

She said quickly, 'Not now.' Then, to Chris, 'Chris, be a love and go into the living room, and get started on your homework, will you? Deedie and I have got to have a talk.'

'What about?' Chris asked, but he stood up and pushed back his chair.

'Never you mind what about. Nothing for you to worry about. You could get in a quarter of an hour's work before tea.'

His look at her said plainly, 'I know when I'm not wanted.' But he left the room. As soon as the door was shut, Stephen said, 'I want to know about my mum.'

'We don't talk about her,' Rose said, uncomfortably.

'Why not?'

'Because of the disgrace.'

'What disgrace? What did she do?'

'You shouldn't be asking me. I'm not going to say. I don't know why you've suddenly started asking questions now, after all this time,' Rose said.

'After all what time? I've always wanted to know what happened to her.'

'I'm not going to talk,' Rose said, and she shut her mouth in a firm thin line.

'You could tell me about her when she was little,' Stephen said.

97

'Why do you want to know about her when she was little?'

He didn't know how to answer this. He said, 'I don't know. I just wondered what she was like when she was a little girl.'

In spite of herself, Rose was smiling. 'She was naughty,' she said.

'Did you get on with her? Or did you and she fight?'

'Fought like devils. About everything.'

'What did she do that was naughty?'

'What didn't she do? Never did as she was told. Ran away more than once.'

'Did you run with her?'

'Me? No. I was the good one, see? It was all I had. Being good, I mean. And pretty. I was prettier than her, and she was jealous.'

Stephen looked at Rose and wondered how she'd managed to be pretty, with that lank pale hair and soft pale face. The face was flabby now, with puffy cheeks and not enough chin, but perhaps when she'd been young she hadn't been pale and puffy.

'Why did she run away?'

Rose was confused. She said, 'She was always difficult to please.'

'What sort of things did you fight about?'

'I said, everything. Clothes. Our mum liked to have us dressed alike, and Margaret wouldn't. If we had things that matched, she'd change them. I remember once she cut a great hole in her new frock and put on a patch out of some red material she'd got from somewhere. I can tell you, our mum was furious. She beat her.'

'Beat her! You mean, with a stick?' Stephen was horrified. He was not surprised his mum had run away.

'With a belt. She was bruised for a week after that.'

'What else did she do?'

98

'Once she painted her face green. And her arms and her neck. Then she went in next door to old Mrs Armitage and told her she was an alien from the stars come to get her.'

'Why did she do that?'

'Mrs Armitage had told on her for climbing over the fence to fetch a ball that had gone in her garden.'

Stephen felt that his mum had certainly not been lacking in spirit. Or in invention. And he had gained something he hadn't known before. His mum had been called Margaret. How ridiculous that her own son hadn't till now known her name!

'Go on.'

'That's all.'

'There must have been a lot more. Who was older, you or her?'

'She was older than me. There was your Aunt Dorothy was the oldest of us girls.'

'Was she naughty too?'

'No. She was the clever one. Got a scholarship to the big school and went into the Civil Service.'

'Is she out here too?' Stephen asked.

'Didn't you see her playing tennis not half an hour ago? Of course she's out here. We all came together. With you.'

'Why did you go to Australia?' He should have asked, 'Why did you come?' but Rose did not notice the mistake.

She stared at him. 'Why? Because of the disgrace, of course. Now, that's enough,' she said, getting up from the table. She called out, 'Chris! You can come back now if you want.' She was bustling about, fetching mugs and plates, preparing for a meal.

Stephen said, 'I wish you'd tell me some more.' But the boy Chris was in the room with them now, and Rose shook her head.

'You'll stay and have some tea?' she asked, but Stephen said, 'No, thanks. I ought to be getting back.' He hoped she wouldn't ask where he was going, as he couldn't have told her anything she would believe. To his relief she allowed him to leave. Probably she was as pleased as he was to end the conversation.

Outside the door he was lost. He hadn't taken notice of the roads along which she had driven him. He walked in what he hoped was the right direction, and finally, despairing, asked a passer-by to direct him to the tennis courts in the park, hoping that there was only one anywhere near. It was a long hot walk, and he was immensely relieved when he saw trees and grass and heard the sound of tennis players hitting balls and calling to each other. Beyond the courts he saw the door he had come through. Gratefully, he turned the key in the lock and escaped. Back to his own world. As he stepped through the door into the little street in his own town, he wondered what would happen if on one of these occasions his key wouldn't open the door and he found himself stuck in that other strange world.

16

The next key that Stephen used was not one from his collection. It did not lead him into another life, it did not provide him with an adventure.

He had been considering how to find out more about his mum. Should he confront his dad by saying, 'I know that my mum's name was Margaret, and I know her family are all living in Australia. Now I want you to tell me why they went out there and what the disgrace was.'? He didn't think his dad would tell him anything. He would simply put on that closed up look and say, 'Stephen, I've told you, I don't want to talk about her.' And that would be that.

If he was ever to find out what had really happened, he would have to find another way. He didn't expect there would be any chance of doing this, but a week or two after his last adventure, Fortune played into his hands. It was a Saturday, so he was at home when his dad rang from the garage to say he hadn't got his keys. Would Stephen look around for them, and would he be there to let him in when he got back that evening?

Stephen found the keys at once. Dad had left them in his room. Something he never usually did, but this morning he wasn't going to work at the garage but was being taken off by George, his friend, to look at another garage which was for sale outside the town. The two of them were going to work out whether they could afford to buy it if they decided it would be a good investment. Stephen hadn't understood whether they wanted to run it

101

instead of the one they already had in town or if it would be an extra. So his dad hadn't needed his car keys and he'd forgotten the lot.

Stephen rang the garage to leave a message for Dad that the keys were safe and that he'd be there to let him in. After which he'd sat down again to go on reading, when it occurred to him to have a look at Dad's keys. There were several in the bunch. The Yale front door key, of course. The two car keys, doors and ignition. Four or five keys to all the garage gates and doors and cupboards and drawers that had to be kept locked when the place was empty. There was the key of the padlock which fastened Dad's one solid piece of luggage, an old brown suitcase, which he never used. There was the key of his desk in the flat. But he never locked it. And there was another key which Stephen didn't recognize. An ordinary key with a rounded top, a long neck and quite a simple pattern of wards.

Like the key of a cupboard or a box or a chest. Or a drawer.

He'd been looking at it for half a minute before he suddenly realized what it was. It was the key to the locked drawer of Dad's little chest.

He looked at it for a much longer time after he'd identified it before he decided to use it. Then, feeling guilty and excited and defiant, he went into Dad's bedroom. Why shouldn't he look inside the drawer? It probably contained nothing he hadn't seen dozens of times before. Dad had never told him not to. If Dad had any guilty secrets, he shouldn't have left his keys lying around where anyone could take them.

He inserted the ordinary key in the lock and opened the drawer. It didn't look promising. There was a bundle of letters, there was an out-of-date diary. Besides these were some yellowing clippings from newspapers, held

102

together by an elastic band. There was a photograph album, much the worse for wear, a tin box labelled 'Capstan Tobacco' and several biros which probably didn't work, judging by their age.

He picked up the tin box, which rattled in a promising way, but when opened showed him only some old coins, dating before decimalization. Large dark pennies, worn thin with use, two sixpences, what he recognized as a half crown, and a folded brown note, which disappointingly turned out to be worth not ten pounds, but ten shillings. Fifty pence. Not exactly treasure trove.

Next he investigated the newspaper clippings. They all dealt with the same subject. A murder. He didn't bother to read the text, just glanced at the headlines and the pictures. WOMAN KILLS ABUSING STEPFATHER, the big type screamed, and MURDER OR MANSLAUGHTER? Stephen wasn't much interested. He wondered why his dad had wanted to keep these cuttings, he had never seemed to want to read this sort of story as long as Stephen could remember. He looked briefly at the pictures. The stepfather was an ordinary sort of bloke, rather good looking in a foxy sort of way. The girl had curly dark hair and, without being beautiful or even pretty, had a face that made you want to look at it again. She looked lively, as if she could have been fun to be with. The pictures, Stephen supposed, had been taken before she was accused of murder, because in most of them she was smiling, or looking serious but as if she might smile at any minute. Someone had blacked out her name all through the article.

He looked at the last cutting to see what had happened to her. She had been found guilty of manslaughter and sentenced to prison for twelve years. He wondered what she looked like now.

He looked at the bundle of letters. But although he was

already looking at what his dad hadn't meant him to see, he baulked at reading his dad's private correspondence. He'd hate it if anyone read what he wrote privately, though that wasn't much. He had once tried to keep a diary, but either it was dead boring or embarrassing, and he'd quickly given it up. The thought of anyone reading what he had written had made him sweat with shame. He pulled the photograph album towards him and looked at the first pages. There was a picture of a house, and underneath it was written '14 Acanthus Grove' and a date seventeen years back. He had an idea that this was where his dad had lived with Gran when he was a young man. There was a figure standing at the open door of the house, but it was too small and indistinct for him to see who it was. Then there were photographs of groups, all of young men. Some of them wore sports gear, so he supposed this was a team his dad had belonged to. Indeed, by looking very closely, he thought he could see Dad in the middle row, looking seriously at the camera. He had had more hair in those days and was larger all round, not fat, but quite well covered. Another group was of school children. Stephen couldn't be sure that he had recognized his dad among those rows of boys, with the meaningless grins children display when the photographer says, 'Smile, please!'

He turned two pages, from which looked people he'd never seen, with his dad's neat writing below the faces of young men with cowlicks, young men with surprisingly long hair, young men and boys looking embarrassed, pleased with themselves, but one or two looked as if they'd been caught unawares and were at ease, natural, not putting on any sort of act.

He came to the next page which was entirely taken up with one large picture of a girl. A girl with dark curling hair, looking at the camera as if she was just about to ask a question. Not a beautiful girl, not even a very pretty girl, but a girl who was immensely alive. In her hand she was holding a flower. A white flower, a very neatly arranged flower, with all its petals in order round the centre, so perfect that it almost might not have been real.

Underneath the portrait his dad had written 'Margaret' and a date.

He put out his hand for the newspaper cuttings. He compared the picture of the murderess with the Margaret in the album. There could be no doubt that they were the same.

He couldn't believe it. He did not want to believe it.

He turned the next page of the album. There was the girl again, with her hair done differently and wearing another outfit, but recognizably the same. She wasn't looking at the camera, this time, but down at the baby in her arms. Underneath this picture his dad's writing read, 'Margaret and Stephen'.

Stephen?

It couldn't be him. He couldn't have a murderess as a mother.

He looked at the date. It was a little after his own birthday. The same year. It was not a stranger that the Margaret was holding.

It was him.

He felt cold. He felt sick.

He put the album back in the drawer together with the bits of old newspaper. He couldn't remember how everything had been placed when he'd first opened the drawer. He just had to hope that his dad wouldn't remember either. He shut and locked the drawer, feeling all the time as if none of this was real. He hadn't opened the drawer, he hadn't read those paragraphs in the newspaper, he hadn't looked in the photograph album. He went to his room and lay on the bed.

He couldn't think straight. What he had seen must add up to some story, but it was a story he didn't want to know. He found that he was saying to himself, 'No! No! It can't be that!' The pictures of the not quite pretty girl kept on coming before his eyes. The posed photographs with his dad's neat writing below. That unforgiving date. The headlines from the newspapers. He tried to push them away, but they always came back. Presently he stood up and walked about his room. It wasn't large enough. He went out into the passage and walked to the kitchen, back to his room, along the passage again, the kitchen again, the passage, his room. He picked up the keys and opened the drawer. Perhaps the whole thing had been a nightmare, none of it was true. But there were the yellowed cuttings, there was the album. He didn't need to examine them again to know what they told him.

He locked the drawer. He felt now that he couldn't care whether or not Dad found out what he had done. He didn't care about anything. He wished that he was dead.

He was still sitting in the kitchen when his dad rang the front door bell. He followed Stephen back into the kitchen.

'Done anything about supper?' he asked.

'No.'

'Put the potatoes on like I told you?'

'No. Sorry.'

'Forgot, did you?'

'Suppose so.' He couldn't stand this. He left the kitchen and shut himself into his own room. He heard the telly spouting the evening news. He heard the door of the fridge shut several times. He lay on his bed and tried not to think. He felt shrunk in misery.

After a long time he heard his dad calling. When he didn't answer, Dad came and looked in at his door.

'Stephen? What's wrong? Not feeling so good?'

'I'm all right,' he made himself say.

'Supper's ready.'

'I don't want any.'

Dad came over and felt his forehead. 'What's wrong, then?'

'I told you. Nothing.'

'If there's nothing, you can come and have something to eat.'

'No.' If he tried to eat, he'd vomit. He knew.

'Gut trouble?'

'I'm not hungry.'

One good thing about Dad was that he didn't waste time on words. Now he said, 'Well, I am. I'll see to you later,' and left.

He was back nearly an hour later. He said, 'I've put your supper in the fridge. It'll be there when you want it.'

He didn't feel as if he would ever want to eat again. He was grateful when Dad left. He went to the bathroom, drank a glassful of cold water and washed his face. Back in his room he lay on the bed again and wondered if he would ever be able to sleep. Then it was dark and he heard his dad opening and shutting doors. He was cold. He pulled a blanket over himself. The next thing he knew, it was morning. He woke as if it was to be another ordinary day, not for a moment recalling what he had learned the day before. Then, like a blow from a great hammer, he remembered. His whole life had been shattered. He did not know how he could live out the rest of it.

17

He did not know what he was going to say to his dad. He knew that somehow he had got to get the answers to the questions he had to ask.

He spent the day rehearsing how to begin. But everything he thought of sounded stupid, and everything struck him as being exactly the sort of thing that his dad would hate. By the time Dad got back from work that evening, Stephen was too anxious and too frightened to know well what he was doing.

Which was perhaps why, as soon as they were sitting over supper, he said, 'Dad! Can I ask you something?'

'What?'

His mouth was dry and he found breathing difficult. 'Was my mum called Margaret?'

Dad looked at him. Stephen saw that he had guessed right. There was a long silence. Then his dad said, 'Why?'

'I wanted to know.'

'You've seen something?'

'I saw the photos.'

'Where? Your aunt?'

He had to confess. 'I looked in that drawer.'

'It's locked.'

'You left your keys here.'

He didn't know what he had expected. Anger? Fury? Punishment? But after another silence, his dad said, 'I suppose you couldn't not.'

He didn't know how to go on.

Dad said, 'I knew you'd have to know some time.'

'What? What happened? She isn't dead, is she?'

'She's not dead. She's in prison.'

'What really happened? Did she . . . ' He couldn't bring himself to say, 'Kill someone'.

'It was her stepfather. He'd always been bad to her. That's why she ran away.'

'Didn't she have a real dad?'

'Went off when she was little. This was a guy her mum brought home.'

'And he was bad to her?'

'First he started on her sister, then her. So she got out. Thought she'd got right away.'

'Hadn't she?'

'Didn't see him for years. Then, one day, he turned up where we were living.'

We? 'Were you there, Dad?'

'Not the day she saw him. At work, wasn't I?'

'You'd married her?'

'Long time before that. You were four. Nearly.'

'Me?'

'You.'

Everything was changing. Had changed. The red and yellow squares of the floor covering were not the colour they had been that morning. The food on his plate was monstrous. He couldn't think that he had ever wanted to eat it. Sound was different. The scrape of Dad's knife on the plate, the tick of the clock, the swish of the passing car, were all strange. He was living in a foreign world. He was an alien, he didn't belong here.

'How'd he know where she was?'

'No idea.'

'Was that when she . . . did it?'

'Not then. He started following her. Then she thought he was going to start on the kid.'

'Start?'

'He was making up to you. Giving you sweets and that. So you'd go to him when you saw him in the street. Or the park.'

'What for? What did he want?'

'To get his own back on her. For getting him thrown out by her mum. And telling on him.'

'She killed him?'

'They said manslaughter. But she had a knife ready next time he came round, so it could have been murder. That's the law. So she got sent down. Twelve years. Should be less with the remission. Say eight.'

'Where?'

'Women's prison. Other side of Redwoods.'

'When . . . when it happened. Where was it?'

'Place called Oakland. Near London.'

'You were living there?'

'Was then. Left directly after. Came here.'

Stephen thought. He asked, 'Did you change our name?'

'Didn't have to. It's a common enough name. Like Smith.'

That was a relief. He didn't want to discover that his name wasn't his own. There were enough other changes he had learned about in the last twenty-four hours.

There were too many questions he ought to ask and couldn't. They sat at the table, neither of them eating or speaking. Outside the sky was darkening. There was a line of pale yellowish light along the western horizon. The rest of the sky was grey.

'She's alive,' Stephen said at last.

'I felt bad letting you think she was dead. But I didn't know how to tell you.'

'Will I ever see her?'

'I'm not taking you to visit her in prison.'

'But . . . will she ever come out?'

'Some time she will.'

'Will she come here?'

His dad said heavily, 'Who knows?' and there was another long silence.

He wanted to know so much that his dad wouldn't want to tell him. What was she really like? What had her stepfather done to her? What had she thought he would do to him, Stephen? What had Dad felt about the whole thing? Had they been happy, married to each other? Did his dad want her back now? When she came out of prison, where would she go? What was he, Stephen, supposed to feel about her? A mother he'd never had. A mother he couldn't remember. A woman who had killed. A murderess.

'You shouldn't worry about it,' his dad said.

Stephen felt like shouting at him. 'What do you expect me to do? Be pleased? Go round telling everyone, "My mum's in prison because she killed someone."?' But he didn't speak.

'You haven't eaten anything,' Dad said.

'I'm not hungry.'

'Mug of tea?'

'No. Thanks.'

Another silence.

'I'm going to bed,' Stephen said.

'Think you'll sleep?'

He didn't think he would be able to, but all he said was, 'Might do.'

He was leaving the room, had almost shut the door behind him, when he heard Dad's voice. 'Stephen!'

'What?'

'Your mum.'

'What?'

'She did what anyone might've done. He was a real bastard.'

Stephen went to his bed. But he did not sleep until the small hours of the next morning.

18

I t was a relief, the next day, to have to go to school. Although at first he felt more than ever a stranger among his friends, as if he was invisibly locked away from them and from everything they thought and talked about, the feeling didn't last. There was too much to do, too much that demanded his attention. For quite long periods he could almost forget his problems, and feel as he had before, the same as his friends.

He knew that Dad was anxious about him. He could almost feel Dad's eyes on him when they were sitting in the same room, over meals, or watching television. For the first few days he was on edge whenever they were together, fearing that Dad was going to start again talking about *that*. But he didn't. The subject seemed to be closed. Stephen certainly wasn't going to re-open it. Luckily, he had recovered some appetite and could manage to eat enough to satisfy his father. They were living together in what looked exactly the same way as they had before. But Stephen knew that his dad knew that he knew that everything now was different.

A week went by. He was sleeping better, though he still sometimes had disturbing dreams. He couldn't always remember them when he woke up, but he knew that they were not agreeable. He wondered how long this state of affairs would go on. Would Dad ever tell him the whole of the story? What would he, Stephen, feel if Dad suddenly said, 'Your mum's coming home tomorrow?' It must happen some time. But he didn't know when. Dad had

113

said that she'd got eight years in prison, with remission, whatever that was. He, Stephen, had been nearly four when she'd been sent there. Now he was twelve, the date of her release must be quite near. He did not want it ever to arrive.

He felt bad about this. Any normal boy, surely, would be longing to see his mum, even if he couldn't remember her? And he couldn't remember her as a person. The figure in the red dress that he'd always thought must have been his mum could have been any woman of about the right age. He had no idea what she was really like. When he'd thought about her before he'd been told the truth, he'd imagined her like the mothers of his friends. He had built up a picture, from those ordinary, friendly women, making her taller than Mrs Betts, prettier than Mike's mum, speaking better than Dan's mum, cleverer than Mrs Richards at school.

What he hadn't added to the figure he'd created was his own mum's history. This new mum was someone with a temper, someone who had been badly used, had run away from home and her own mother. Had killed someone. There were moments which horrified him, when he was proud of what she'd done. As if the deed had made her a sort of heroine. There were other moments when he was ashamed and angry with her. She shouldn't have put him in this position. She should have been ordinary, like the others. She should have been there for him. She shouldn't have left him to live with Dad, who spoke so little and who never showed his feelings. Dad, as far as he could remember, had never hugged him, almost never said anything affectionate. They had lived not like father and son, but like two strangers who just happened to be under the same roof. Dad had looked after him, had provided food and clothes and things like his toys when he was little and his bike and entertainments. But it had all seemed as if Dad did these things because he knew that that was what fathers did, not because he wanted to. If Stephen had ever used the word, which he didn't, even to himself, he would have said that what he missed was what Dad did not appear to be able to give him. Something like affection.

The days went on apparently just as usual. Stephen went to school, sat in class, sometimes learning, sometimes not, played football, did his homework, watched the telly, did all the things he had always done. But with a difference. Nothing was really the same. If he'd been able to pretend that they were during the day, the nights would have denied it. He dreamed now every night, anxious dreams in which he couldn't get to some place in time, he hadn't done his school work for some examination, or he had to make some extraordinary effort, jumping over a gulf, running a distance, climbing a rockface, and he couldn't bring himself to start. There were near nightmares too, when he had committed some crime which would soon be discovered, or an unknown danger was lurking in familiar but now terrifying places. The worst took place in his own home. Behind a door which should have been well known and unthreatening, was a figure which must not be set free. He was in the passage, trying to lock the door. The key wouldn't go into the lock, then, when at last he'd got it in, it wouldn't turn. He saw the door handle moved from the other side, it turned and the door groaned as it began to open.

'You all right?' his dad asked one morning at breakfast after one of these troubled nights.

'All right,' was all that Stephen would say. But he wasn't.

He knew he was bottling things up. That was why they came to attack him at night. But there was no one he could talk to. He did once get as far as saying to Dad, 'About

115

my mum. How much longer . . . ?' but Dad said, 'I'll tell you when you need to know,' and left the room. Stephen knew that there was no hope there. He had even wondered whether to try talking to Aunt Alice. But he knew that wouldn't be any use. He couldn't possibly tell any of his friends. There was no one he could trust even to listen. The secret had to remain locked up inside himself.

At one point he even thought of Miss Oddie. Why? He had no idea. But once the thought had come into his head, it returned again and again. Sitting in her kitchen, peeling potatoes, he might almost have been able to speak. She wouldn't have interrupted. He thought she wouldn't have been shocked. He wished he could go back to Martelsea to try the experiment. But when he played the imaginary scene over in his head, he knew he couldn't. Ring her front door bell—what would he say? 'I've come to tell you something I can't tell anyone else. My mum is alive and she's in prison. She killed someone.'

Impossible.

It was November. Days were short, the sun was cool, trees were turning copper and gold, the pavements were slippery with leaves. On a Saturday, when he was sitting in the kitchen struggling with an essay, the doorbell rang. When he answered it he saw Alex.

She said, 'Hi!'

'Hi!'

'Haven't seen you for ages.'

'I didn't know you were here.'

'Haven't been till this weekend.'

They stood looking at each other.

'Can I come in?' she asked.

He led the way to the kitchen.

'I haven't been here before. Is that your homework?'

'I've got to write about the best and the worst books I've ever read.'

'That'd be fun. What are they?'

'The worst was some soppy thing about a dog that learned to talk.'

'I've read that one. I hated it. But it wasn't my worst. What's your best?'

'Haven't decided yet. What was your worst?'

'I'll think.' He thought she looked funny, standing there in a bright bar of sunlight which slanted across the room.

She said, 'I think it was a book about a girl called Angela who went round being good. Everything that happened to her, she always said wasn't too bad because of something or other. Like if it rained when she was out for the day, she used to say how lovely for the flowers. Things like that.'

'Ugh!'

'That's what I thought. And then her mum died, and she said it was really a good thing because her mum would be living with the angels and wouldn't be in pain any more.'

'Was she in pain? When she was alive, I mean?'

'I can't remember. I didn't read it properly, it was too stupid. I suppose she was, or horrible Angela wouldn't have said it.'

The conversation seemed to Stephen to be becoming dangerous. He said, 'Would you like some tea?'

'What about your homework?'

'I've got time.'

He made the mugs of tea. He was surprised to find that he was pleased to see Alex. If he'd been asked before she appeared, he'd have said he never wanted to see her again.

'Biscuit?'

'Please.'

'We've only got digestive. Unless there's a custard cream underneath.'

There was, but only one. They bickered agreeably about who should have it, and finally shared it.

'You've given me the bigger half.'

'There's no such thing as a bigger half.'

'What d'you mean?'

'If it's a half, it's half. It can't be bigger than the other half or it wouldn't be a half, would it?' When she laughed, her eyes screwed up. He rather liked the way she looked. Japanesey.

'Have you had any more of those key adventures?'

'Had one.' But he wasn't going to tell her about it.

'What happened?'

'Nothing much. Saw some people playing tennis.'

'That all? But you've still got the keys?'

'Yes.'

She said seriously, 'If there was something you wanted to know about that's going on in that other life, you might be able to get to where it is and see what it's like.'

He thought at once about his mother. Meeting her.

'Couldn't you?' Alex was saying.

'I don't know.'

'What's the matter?'

'Nothing,' he said, angry.

'There is, though. Has something happened? Did you have another adventure and it was really bad?'

'No.'

'Something's happened. You're different.'

'I'm not.'

'You are. You're sort of . . . sad. No, that's not right. I feel as if you'd gone a long way away and you don't want to get back.'

He didn't answer this.

'If it wasn't something to do with your keys, it's something that's happened now. Real.'

Yes, it was real enough.

118

'I wish you'd tell me. I wouldn't be able to do anything, but if you told me you'd feel better. That's what my mum says. And it's true.'

'Just telling someone?'

'Someone you like, of course.'

'Oh! Like!'

'I'd understand if you don't like me enough. I know you didn't after you'd gone through that door in the street.'

'I do like you. Quite,' he said.

'Well, then?'

But he wasn't going to. Whatever her mum said, he didn't believe that telling her would make him feel better. It couldn't alter the facts. She must have seen from his closed look that he wasn't going to talk. She got up and said, 'I'll be off, then.'

He saw her to the door. She said, 'Thanks for the tea.'

'That's all right.'

'You could tell me. I wouldn't ever tell anyone else.'

He was pleased when she was gone.

19

After this Stephen sat on his bed, with his bedroom door locked. He wanted to be able to think without being disturbed.

Alex had been right. When he went through one of those doors, he found himself with his mum's family. As if he'd been taken with them when they'd left England. That wouldn't be an extraordinary 'If'. He decided that this was something he could ask Dad right away. He'd be back to supper, though late, because it was a Saturday. He knew that if he left it too long, he'd never have the courage to start speaking of his mum again.

He waited till nearly the end of the meal, and then he began. 'Dad! Are they in Australia? My mum's family?'

Dad looked startled. He said, 'Why?'

'Because you said something about them being the other side of the world. So I thought perhaps it was Australia.'

His dad said, 'Yes, they're in Australia.'

'When did they go there?' Stephen asked.

'After the trial. Wanted to get right away. There was an uncle there already. And your mum's brother.'

'So I could have gone there too?'

'What made you think of that?' Dad asked. Now it was happening. Dad looked as if he might be going to get angry.

'Just wondered,' Stephen said. He thought this sounded feeble, so he added, 'I wondered what it would be like.'

'Can't tell you. I've never been,' Dad said.

'Did you think of going?'

'No, I didn't. Why should I? I didn't ever get on that well with your mum's family. I wouldn't have wanted to be with them wherever they were.'

So this hadn't been one of those 'If' situations, Stephen thought. Alex was wrong. But his dad suddenly said, 'They wanted to take you, though.'

'Why didn't they, then?'

'I didn't let them, did I?'

'You mean, you wanted to keep me here? With you?'

'They tried hard. God knows why. They hadn't treated your mum that well when she was with them. Felt guilty about her, I daresay.'

'How did they try hard?' Stephen asked.

'Said I'd never be able to manage with a kid on my own. There was a lot of sob stuff about how kids ought to be with their mum's family. Bullshit, it was. I knew I could manage quite as well as them. Better. They tried to get at you to say you'd rather go off with them, too.'

'I don't remember,' Stephen said.

'You weren't much more than a baby. But I knew what was best for you. They're a poor lot. Your mum was the only one of them who had any brains. Or any spirit.'

Stephen considered this. If the people he'd met behind those doors were really his mum's family, he couldn't contradict his dad's view of them. He hadn't particularly liked them. In fact he'd found the way they'd treated him somehow cloying. They were too affectionate, it didn't quite ring true. But what struck him more than this was the fact that his dad hadn't wanted to let him go. In spite of the fact that it must have been tough for him having a kid to look after when that kid was really small. It struck him, for almost the first time, that perhaps his dad had actually been fond of him. Didn't just regard him as something to be put up with and corrected, but had wanted to have him around. It was such an amazing idea that he didn't feel he could say any more just then. That suited his dad all right. Never one to say more on any subject than was absolutely necessary, Dad had now picked up the evening paper and was glancing at it in the way he had of not quite reading it seriously, but indicating that he was preparing to get lost in it if there were no more questions.

Stephen would have liked to make sure that he'd guessed right, by asking, 'Did you really want to have me living here?' But he couldn't. And he knew that if he did, Dad's answer was likely to be something offhand, like 'Didn't know what you'd turn out like, did I?' Something unsatisfactory. Dad was never going to come out with a straight declaration of—what did Stephen want? Approval? Affection? Why not say, straight out, love?

20

It was December and the end of term was within sight. There was the usual carol concert, and a play done by the seniors, which Stephen enjoyed more than he'd expected. He hadn't thought that *The Winter's Tale* by that well-known writer, William Shakespeare, could possibly tell him anything he wanted to know, or find interesting. He was not really involved in the story until it had reached Bohemia and the finding of Perdita, and when, at the end, Hermione was proved not to have died, though he couldn't believe that she'd been kept hidden for so long, he was intrigued. A mother, come back from the dead. It was a stupid story, full of unlikely events, but that part of it could be true for him.

During the short Christmas holiday he was going to have the usual problem. He had to find a present for his dad, always a nightmare. If asked, Dad always said he didn't want anything, 'So don't go wasting your money.' But this year, especially, Stephen wanted to give Dad something he'd really like. He wanted it to be expensive, too, and that raised another problem. He hadn't much cash. He tried to get a job. There were boys not much bigger than him who were temporary postmen, but when he asked at the Post Office, he was told that sixteen was the minimum age. He had to find out if anyone wanted a short term paper-boy. At first, he despaired. At each place he asked, he was told they'd got all the regular boys they needed and that anyway he'd have to be thirteen, or they couldn't legally employ him. But at the fifth shop, he was lucky. One of their delivery boys had just gone off sick. 'Influenza. So he won't be back much before Christmas,' the shop woman said, gloomily. She looked Stephen over with suspicion and not only asked how old he was, but also said that he must bring a reference. Stephen added a couple of months to his real age, and suggested the name of his form master, hoping that Mr Bates would not remember that he wasn't yet quite thirteen. He was relieved when he was told, a day later, that he'd got the job. The wages were not magnificent, but would bring in enough to make him feel that this time he'd be able to find something really good, something Dad would know must have taken time and trouble to find. It was convenient that the paper-round started so early that he could combine it with being at school. He did it for three weeks and was grateful that he wouldn't always have to get out of bed at that cold dark hour of the morning.

He took the train to London. Surely there he'd find something his dad would like. He was tired by the time he'd trudged through what felt like hundreds of shops, looking. He'd seen shirts he'd have liked for himself, but which Dad probably wouldn't be seen dead in. He'd looked at shelves and shelves of books, but couldn't find anything he was sure that Dad would read. He had pored over the windows of jewellers' shops, wondering whether Dad would wear those comic cufflinks—but he didn't wear the sort of cuffs that required links. He had wandered through the menswear departments and seen innumerable ties, scarves, pullovers, pyjamas. It was while he was in one of these, that he suddenly remembered his dad saying, not long ago, 'I'll have to get rid of this old cardigan. It's got holes all over, and the buttons aren't anything to write home about.' It was a shapeless brown garment that Dad had worn at home after it had served its purpose at work. So a new cardigan was something he really needed. Stephen started with renewed vigour on his quest.

It couldn't be anything with a pattern. And at first all the cardigans Stephen looked at had patterns of one kind or another, or their colours were too bright. He wandered from shop to shop, and began to feel depressed as well as exhausted, when he saw exactly what he wanted in the window of a small shop that sold nothing but knitwear. It was light brown and absolutely plain. It had dark brown buttons, nothing fancy. As Stephen looked at it through the window, he could imagine his dad wearing it. It was absolutely right for him. Feeling pleased that at last he'd found what he wanted, he went into the shop.

The first thing that went wrong was the assistant who came forward to serve him. When Stephen asked about the cardigan in the window, the man said, 'Nothing like that in your size, sonny.'

Stephen hated being called 'sonny'. He said, coldly, 'It's not for me. It's for my dad.'

The man said, 'What size did you want then?' sounding more interested. Fortunately Stephen knew the answer to this. The man pulled open a drawer and took out a pile of cardigans, looking through them for the right size. When he had found it, he laid it reverently on the counter, and said, 'A very superior article. You won't find anything to equal this however far you look.'

Stephen had to agree. It was perfect, absolutely right as a very special present. What was not absolutely right was the price. When Stephen heard it, he was shocked. He had never dreamed that a perfectly plain cardigan could cost so much. 'It's pure cashmere,' the shop assistant was saying, and he stroked the garment fondly, to show how valuable and soft it was.

Stephen did a quick, desperate calculation. The sum was more than he had, but it wasn't that much more than

125

he could earn by the end of the week if he stuck to the newsround. He hadn't meant to. He had meant to leave and have some time with Mick, who had a new computer game which he'd invited Stephen to try. And there must surely be other cardigans which would look very much like this one but which wouldn't be pure cashmere and not cost so much. He asked. Yes, there were other plain cardigans, and the man got one out to show. Stephen was tempted. It was a perfectly all right garment, the sort Dad always bought for himself. But it was nothing out of the ordinary and Stephen wanted this present to be special. He said, 'I haven't got enough money on me now, but I could have most of it by next Monday. Would you keep it for me till then, and I'll come back?'

The assistant looked doubtful. He said, 'What d'you mean, you'll have most of it?'

'I'll have earned almost as much as that. I'll get the rest somehow.' He didn't know how he would do this. He might just possibly be able to borrow from Mick.

The assistant said, 'Pity you have to purchase the article now. After Christmas we'll be reducing the prices of most of our stock. Why don't you come back next month?'

Stephen said, 'I can't do that. It's for a Christmas present.'

'For your dad?' the man asked.

'Yes. And I've got to be able to give it to him on the day.'

The assistant said, 'Wait here a moment,' and disappeared into a back room, taking the pile of cardigans with him. Did he think that Stephen was going to walk off with them? He reappeared almost at once and said, 'Mr Borrodale says it will be all right to let you have the cardigan next week at its sale price. Only you mustn't tell your friends, or we shall have them all coming and asking for the discount.'

126

'I won't tell anyone,' Stephen said, immensely relieved. He thought he could forgive the man for that 'sonny'. The sale price, when he was told it, was only a pound or two more than he would have by the following week, if he added his savings to what he would have earned.

He went home, feeling pleased and sorry. Pleased that he'd found exactly the right present for Dad and sorry that it meant he wouldn't have more than about fifty pence to last him till he got his pocket money at the end of next week.

He finished the week at the newsagent's, was paid, and confirmed at home that with what he'd been able to save earlier, he had just enough to pay for the cashmere cardigan. On Monday, he went back to London and bought it. It had been beautifully packed in a slim box and sheets and sheets of tissue paper. Stephen realized that it had been a very expensive shop, not the kind he or his dad ever went into. He hugged himself with anticipation of what his dad would feel when he saw this magnificent garment. Then he reminded himself that Dad was never one to show what he was feeling. It was unlikely that he'd say more than 'Thanks. It's great.' But he would know and Stephen would know that the cardigan represented something new in their relationship.

A few days before Christmas, Alex knocked again at the door. Stephen let her in, and took her into the kitchen. It hadn't occurred to him to get anything to give her, and he was already feeling embarrassed that he hadn't so much as a card for her, when she said, 'I just came to say Happy Christmas!'

'Same to you,' Stephen said.

'And I've brought you a sort of present.'

She saw his face fall and said hurriedly, 'It's not a proper present. I didn't go out and buy it. It's just something my mum had and I thought you might like it.'

Stephen said, 'I'm afraid I didn't . . .'

'No, you shouldn't have. But I saw this in one of Mum's cupboards and I thought, as you're collecting them, you might like it. Though it's fairly horrible to look at.'

She held out a key. It was large and dark and somehow rather forbidding. Stephen took it from her. It was immensely heavy and it was much the largest key he'd had. He said, 'Doesn't your mum want it?'

'No. It's ages old. She said it came from a barn that was on the farm her dad had, when she was little. She didn't remember why she'd kept it. But when I said you were collecting keys . . . sort of . . . she said I could have it in case you'd like it.'

Stephen said, 'You didn't tell her . . . ?'

'Of course not. I just said you had a sort of collection of keys and could I have it to ask you if you'd like it.'

'Thanks.' Stephen felt as tongue-tied as his dad.

'That's all.'

'Thanks. And thank your mum too.'

'She didn't want it.'

'I'm sorry I haven't anything for you.'

'Don't be silly. I don't want anything.'

'Are you staying here over Christmas?'

'No. My dad's coming with the car to fetch Mum's uncle to spend Christmas with us. So he won't be here all alone. It's going to be terrible having him, but Mum said we must.'

'Why is it going to be terrible?'

'Because he forgets everything. He'll put everything in the wrong places and we won't be able to find them for weeks.'

'How long are you here for, then?'

'Going this evening. That's why I came round now.'

There was a long pause.

128

It was several minutes before Alex said, hesitantly, 'I think I've guessed what was wrong that time last month when you didn't want to tell me.'

Could she have? He hoped she couldn't. He said, 'I don't want to talk about it now, either.'

She took no notice. 'Your dad's told you about your mum, hasn't he?'

'What do you mean?' he asked, angry and frightened.

'He's told you that she's dead.'

Before he meant to, he had cried out, 'No!'

'She isn't dead?'

'No.'

'You mean she left you? When you were a baby?'

This was worse. 'She didn't want to.'

'Is she ill? In hospital or something?'

There could be only one reason for someone being in hospital all that time. He said, 'She isn't in a madhouse, if that's what you mean.'

She began, 'I don't understand . . . '

He said, violently, 'Why don't you leave me alone?'

'I'm sorry. I thought it might help.'

He was too angry to speak. He turned and pushed her away and she half fell sideways. He was pleased. But when she stood up again, he saw that she had cut her cheek against the corner of the kitchen dresser. He had cut his own face on that corner before now. He could see blood running down from the wound. She was pulling out a handkerchief to staunch it, but drops were falling on to her sweater. He was no longer pleased, he was appalled. He took out his own handkerchief, fortunately almost unused, and handed it to her. She said, 'Thanks.'

'I'm sorry.'

She didn't answer.

'I'm really sorry.'

He saw that she was trying not to cry. He wondered

129

how much damage he had done. Could she have broken a bone in her face? He said, 'Does it hurt a lot?'

'It hurts a bit.'

'Do you think anything's broken?'

She felt the cheek with cautious fingers. 'No. It's just the skin.'

Relief. He said again, 'I'm sorry. I don't know why I did that.'

'You were angry with me.'

'I'm not now.'

'You've got a terrific temper.'

'I've said I'm sorry.'

'All right. I'm sorry I went on about it.'

They sat for another minute or two without speaking. Then Stephen said, 'Oughtn't you to get it cleaned up?'

'Suppose I should.'

'I think we've got something Dad used to put on me when I got hurt.'

'All right. I don't know where Uncle Joe keeps that sort of thing.'

In the tiny bathroom, he told her to wash her face with soap. Then she dabbed the wound with the antiseptic. 'Ow! Stings!' she said. It was no longer bleeding, but a dark blue bruise was already beginning to show.

'What'll you say when your mum asks how you did it?' Stephen asked.

She looked in the glass over the basin. 'I'll say I walked into a lamp-post. Isn't that what drunks always say?'

'She won't believe you.'

'Then I'll say I got punched by a friend.' She was laughing at him, and he didn't mind.

'Funny sort of friend she'll think you have.'

'I'll think of something. Don't worry. I won't tell her it was you.'

'I am sorry,' he said, and meant it.

130

'All right. You don't have to go on saying that.'

'Tea?' he said.

Back in the kitchen he made mugs of tea. He ladled the sugar into hers. He knew about people in shock. She seemed all right, though, drinking the too-hot liquid in loud gulps.

He said, 'Why did you go on? About my mum?'

She said, 'Because I know something bad has happened about her. I thought it might help if you said what it was. After all, it can't be worse than her leaving you. Or being dead.'

Couldn't it? There wasn't time to weigh up the different possibilities, but he had a feeling that she might be right. His mum wasn't dead, she hadn't deserted him. A great many instant thoughts flashed through his mind. Then he decided. She knew so much already, it was better to tell her the lot. He said, 'I'd always thought my mum was dead.'

'And she isn't after all. Where is she?'

He told her. By degrees, he told her everything. She sat looking at him, not interrupting except to ask a question when she didn't understand. She asked the same questions that he had asked his dad, and he couldn't answer them. When he'd finished, she said, 'Poor you.'

It was the sympathy that made his eyes water and the lump come in his throat. He swallowed and said, 'So I don't know what's going to happen.'

'When she comes out?'

'That's right.'

'Aren't you pleased she'll be around? After all this time?'

He was angry again. 'How can I be pleased? I don't know her, what she's like. I might not like her.'

'She's your mum!'

'Not really, she isn't. She hasn't been my mum all these years, has she? She'll be like a stranger.'

'I'd be pleased if it was my mum coming back.'

'Even if she'd . . . whatever she'd done?'

She almost shouted at him, 'Yes!'

'But you know yours. What she's like as a person. I don't know what mine's like. I only know she killed someone.'

'You said your dad said he was a nasty piece of work?'

'But you can't go round killing anyone who's a nasty piece of work.' Stephen thought of several people at school who fitted this description and suddenly he laughed.

'What are you laughing at?'

'Thinking of Beve at school. He's the nastiest piece of work I know.'

She sat silent. Then she said, 'Couldn't you use one of your keys to find out?'

'Find out what?'

'What your mother's really like.'

'How?'

'Go to somewhere where she's around and talk to her.' He noticed that she hadn't said the word prison.

'Every time I've used a key I've been in Australia. She's somewhere in England. I don't see that that's going to be a lot of help.'

'You don't think you might be able to choose?'

'I've never known where I was going to be with any of the keys. I don't choose, do I?'

'You've never tried.'

It was true. But he didn't want to.

'How many keys have you got that you haven't tried yet?'

'Just the one you've just given me.'

'Why don't you try? Getting to see her? Your mum.'

'I might.' He was tired of this conversation. He wanted Alex to leave.

As if she'd heard his wish, she drank her tea quickly. She got up and said, 'I'll be off, then.' He saw her to the door. She said, 'Thanks for the tea.'

'That's all right.'

She was gone. He wasn't sure whether he was glad he'd told her, or not.

21

Perhaps Alex's mum had been right. Stephen reluctantly admitted to himself that it had been a relief to talk. And he had also to admit that he couldn't have found anyone better to talk to. Alex hadn't reacted badly. She hadn't seemed particularly shocked, she hadn't turned soppy about mothers in general, she had asked the same questions that he had asked of his dad. He began to feel that next time she was visiting next door, he'd talk to her again.

Meanwhile ordinary life went on. He began to forget. Or rather, he never completely forgot, but he was able to think about other things for quite long periods at a time. Football. School work. To his own astonishment, he found that he was quite interested in the science lessons which were new that term. It intrigued him to learn that 'metals' were not, as he'd always thought, things like gold bars and silver coins and tin cans and iron posts, but atoms of chemical substances which each had its own peculiar properties. Different from non-metals. He liked the idea of these atoms linking on to each other in their billions to make what could actually be seen with the naked eye. It gave him the feeling that what he saw in everyday life and what he had always accepted as just what it looked like, was really a whole unknown world of fizzing activity. The thought made him mentally dizzy. But he found that he could hold both ideas at once. Here was the kitchen table at which he sat and ate and on which he spread his books and papers, and at the same time, here was a centre of energy, all those tiny particles rushing together to make—wood. Which had once been alive, a tree. He supposed that everything in the world was made up of as many different explanations. So that you could never look at anything simply again. You only saw what it was being for you at this moment. A millionth part of its whole existence.

It was deepest winter. On rainy mornings he seemed to be going to school in the dark and it was dusk when he came home. He was growing suddenly immensely fast. Dad grumbled when he had to buy new boots, new shoes, new trousers and jacket. 'I can't help it, can I?' Stephen complained.

'Hope you slow down soon,' Dad said. But he didn't stop Stephen choosing the shirts and trousers he wanted, even when they were not the cheapest. 'Just make them last,' he said.

They seemed to be on the usual terms. A sort of unexpressed cool friendship. Dad mostly silent, more often out than at home, hardly ever asking questions about Stephen's daily occupations, not talking about his own.

And between them was always the unexpressed question of when? Where? How? Stephen knew that the time for his mother's release from prison must be near. But he did not ask and his dad never spoke of it.

It was because he could think of nothing he wanted to do, that on the last weekend before Christmas he looked again at the keys. Was it possible that, as Alex had suggested, he might be able to learn what sort of a mother he would have? He took the key Alex had given him and examined it. It was the largest he had had, and with its long straight stem and the loop at the top, it looked somehow formal. A severe key. The wards were simple. Straightforward. An official key. Not made for fantasy.

135

Because he couldn't think of anything else to do, he put it in his pocket and went out on his bike. He rode away from the town. It didn't take very long to be out in what was almost country. The road was bordered by hedges, there were fields on either side, and the houses were few and far between. He cycled on, not caring where he went, wondering occasionally whether he was going to be able to find his way back. There was no sun to steer by, the sky was grey and woolly, and he had very little idea in which direction he was going. Presently he came to a village. There was a village green with several houses round it, a church with a small crowded churchyard, and two immense chestnut trees, now almost bare of leaves, near a duck pond. There was nothing to tempt him to stop. He rode on. He passed a farm and saw a yard full of farm machinery. An old man called out to him, 'Where're you off to?'

Stephen called back, 'Don't know,' and hurried on. He did not want to stop and talk.

Presently the hedge on one side of the road gave way to a high stone wall. It had curved iron spikes on top of it, and he wondered what the owner was so anxious to keep out. When he came to a gate, he dismounted and went to peer through the bars to see what was so precious inside. He saw a long drive bordered by dark trees, leading uphill. It disappeared round the side of the hill. He couldn't see any house.

He rode on further and came to another gate. He tried to spy through this one too, but the bars were backed by metal sheeting. He could see nothing. Annoyed, he rattled the gate, but it was too heavy to move. It was taller than the first he had seen and immensely solid. Which was perhaps why, when he saw a gaping keyhole below his left hand, he thought of his last key and tried it in the lock. It won't work, he thought. This immense gate hadn't given him the feeling he'd had about the other doors he'd been through. It wouldn't have anything to do with him. It wouldn't be Australia he would find himself in.

He was surprised when the key turned. He pushed the gate open, and found that he was looking up a short drive towards a huge turreted building of red brick with white facings and many small windows, all barred. In the middle of the frontage was a high arch, guarded by a large wooden door. Not a grand mansion, like those he'd seen in television dramas, more like a sham castle. He didn't like it. It was pretending to be something it wasn't.

As he looked he saw that a part of the large door was a smaller door, and that it was opening. Three people came out, a uniformed man with keys in his hand, followed by two women, one carrying small hand luggage. They walked down the gravel path towards the gate. Stephen just had time to hide himself between the bushes growing inside the high wall. He heard keys rattling but he remained hidden.

The two women were speaking to the man, saying goodbyes. Now that they were near him, he could hear what they said to each other. They did not have the Australian accent he had heard in his earlier experiences. It was plain English like his own.

One of the women said, 'It was good of you to come. Specially today.'

The other said, 'I wasn't doing anything today, anyway.'

The first woman said, 'Still, I'm grateful. You didn't have to come yourself.'

'We always do send someone. For anyone who's been in a long time.'

The first woman said, 'It has seemed long. It's difficult to believe it's finished with.'

'It'll take time to acclimatize,' the second woman said, and the first replied, 'I know.'

They stood for a short time not speaking. Then the second woman said, 'The car was supposed to be here.'

'I don't mind. It's good to be in the fresh air.'

There was another silence. Then the second woman said, 'Your husband?'

'I don't know.'

'You weren't expecting him to be here?'

She answered 'No.' She said it neutrally. No blame. Not even sadness.

'Do you think there's a future for you with him?'

'I've no idea.'

'He hasn't said?'

'No.'

They were silent again. Then the first woman said, 'There's the boy.'

'Yes. I wasn't thinking. How old is he?'

'Growing up.'

'He knows?' the second woman asked gently.

'My husband told him. Not so long ago.'

'And . . . ?'

'I don't know.'

'How old was he when . . . '

'Four. Nearly.' She said suddenly, 'Deedie.'

She was his mother. Peering through the leaves of the bush, he could see now that she wasn't unlike the photographs. She had the same dark curling hair, but her face was thinner and had lines which hadn't been there before. She had a closed in, almost secretive expression. But when she looked round at the frozen road and the leafless trees, she smiled, and Stephen saw at once that what she had not lost was the liveliness and friendliness which had shone out of those early pictures.

The second woman said, 'Here it is,' and Stephen heard the sounds of a car coming along the road and drawing up in front of the gates. He heard a voice say, 'Sorry I'm

138

late. Traffic was really bad.' Then the sound of doors being opened and slammed shut. He heard the clang of the big gate and the turning of the key in the lock. Then the footsteps of the man going back up the drive to the red brick fortress.

Stephen waited till he thought the man would have reached the wooden door. Then he dared to come out from behind the sheltering bushes. He unlocked the big gate and came out on to the deserted road.

He picked up his unnoticed bicycle and rode home. There was very little traffic now, but he lost his way several times. His dad was annoyed that he'd come in so late. He did not ask where he had been, and if he had, Stephen would have found it hard to tell him.

22

He had seen his mother.
What surprised him was how ordinary she had seemed.

He must have been expecting something quite different. A woman who looked as if she could kill. That still young woman in a winter coat and bare head, talking in a quiet voice to the visitor who had come to meet her, could have been anyone he might pass in the street and not notice. She wasn't anything like his idea of a murderess. This was the end of another of his imaginings. He realized that he had been building up a picture of their meeting in which he had recognized something from a long way past. He had wondered if he would find her voice familiar. Or perhaps it would be the way she walked that would bring back memories he didn't know he had. But this wasn't the case. She was a stranger. He felt nothing for her, only discomfort for himself. He did not want her to be part of his family. He and Dad were all right as they were, in the cool, detached relationship they had shared for the last eight or nine years. She would be an unnecessary extra. And he was afraid that she might somehow put him to shame by appearing in their lives, and making it necessary for him to have to account for her long absence to people he knew. He wished guiltily that she would never come out of prison. As long as she stayed locked up, she was no threat, but once she had come out, he thought he could never be easy again.

It was the next day that his dad said, 'We'll be going over to see your gran on Christmas Day.'

Stephen said, 'Do we have to?'

'You know we do.'

'I hate going there.'

'I don't like it much, myself,' Dad said.

'Let's not, then. We could stay here. There's always lots to watch on the telly.'

'We won't stay long.'

'Do we have to go for Christmas dinner?'

'Alice won't like it if we don't.'

'Her cooking's horrible.'

He knew that his dad agreed, though he didn't say anything.

'Couldn't we skip dinner? For once?'

'No, we couldn't. And you've to look as if you were eating.'

'I bet Gran wouldn't notice if I didn't.'

'Alice would. No. We're going. That's all about it.'

Stephen had a feeling that there was something not being said. He was right. After a long pause, his dad said, 'Your mum'll be coming out after Christmas.'

He almost said, 'I know.' But stopped himself in time.

'She won't be coming here, though,' Dad said.

'Where?'

'There's places they take people to when they first come out. Gives them a chance to get used to it.'

'What sort of places?'

'Halfway houses, they're called. Or something stupid like that.'

Stephen made himself ask, 'Will she be coming here?'

'Not for a long time. If ever.'

He would have liked to ask what would decide whether she came here or not. But it was the sort of question his

141

dad certainly wouldn't answer. Instead, he asked, 'You going to see her?'

'I've been seeing her. Every month.'

'I mean, when she comes out.'

'Depends what she wants.'

He couldn't make out what his dad felt. Did he want that woman back? Did he still think of her as his wife? Why couldn't he say what he was feeling instead of this locked up silence that shut out Stephen and the rest of the world? Stephen dared to say, 'What do *you* want?'

To his surprise, Dad didn't answer the question at once with one of his put-down replies that didn't tell you a thing. He seemed to be thinking. Then, at last, he said, 'It's been a long time. We'll have to see.'

Stephen blurted out, 'What about me?'

'What about you?'

'Doesn't she want to see me?' He remembered the way the woman by the leaded gate had said, 'Deedie!' He had been able then to see that this thin, older woman was the same as the young, eager one in the photographs. What he couldn't fit into the picture was that she was in prison because she had killed someone.

His dad said, 'She's asked about you. Every time I saw her.'

He didn't know why this made him feel choked. He managed to say, 'She didn't want to see me?'

'I wouldn't take you there. Not to see her like that.'

'But when she comes out?'

'We'll see.'

He didn't know what he wanted. A mother who had been in prison? A mother he hadn't seen for more than eight years? A mother he couldn't remember? Would she expect him to be all loving and cuddly as he must have been when he was a baby? It was all confusing and uncomfortable. He wished his mum had died instead of being alive now. Then he felt bad at wishing that. But he was still angry with her. He knew that it wasn't exactly her fault that she was going to be around any minute now to upset the ordinary life he'd lived ever since he could remember. He was used to being Stephen with just a dad and no mother, and that was how he wanted it to go on.

23

Christmas was over. Aunt Alice's Christmas dinner had been more than usually dreadful. Gran had been demanding and whiny and sorry for herself. Her present to Dad had been an unwearable scarf knitted by herself, and to Stephen she had given a very old leather purse with a broken fastening. 'It's not new, but there's plenty of wear in it yet,' she had said.

'I shall throw it away when we get home,' Stephen said as they drove away from that sad house, where Gran complained and Aunt Alice suffered.

'Belonged to my dad,' Stephen's father said.

'Do you want me to keep it, then?'

'Not if it's no use.'

'You don't want it?'

'No. Thanks.'

Stephen had saved the cardigan to give Dad after they'd got back. He'd felt it would be something to look forward to, to help him get through the visit to Gran. He knew that his dad wouldn't want to have to open that elegant box and all the tissue paper inside. Opening the wrappings of presents was one of the things that deeply embarrassed him, so Stephen took the cardigan out of its box and handed it to Dad, naked, as you might say.

'Here. My present for you,' Stephen said, wondering whether Dad could possibly appreciate its importance. He watched as Dad slowly unfolded the arms of the cardigan, his expression giving nothing away. He held it up against himself. Then, he took off the pullover he was wearing and put on the cardigan. Stephen was pleased to see that it was a perfect fit. Dad still didn't speak. There was a small mirror that lived permanently behind a mug on the kitchen dresser. Dad pulled it out and looked at himself. Then, at last, he looked at Stephen and said, 'Thanks. Looks good, don't you think?'

Stephen said yes, he did.

Dad stroked the sleeve of the cardigan and said, 'Cashmere?'

'It's cashmere,' Stephen said.

'I've never had anything cashmere,' Dad said.

'It'll be warm,' Stephen said.

'I'll be as grand as the Great Mogul,' Dad said. Passing Stephen on his way back to his usual chair, he put out a hand and just touched Stephen's hair. He didn't say any more, but Stephen was satisfied. Dad had understood.

The week after Christmas and before the New Year was as might have been expected. Stephen watched television more than usual because most of the big shops were shut and most of his friends were away. He was bored. But at the same time he was uneasy. In a few days' time, his mother would be coming out of that red brick prison he had seen. She would be free. Free to visit him. He dreaded the moment.

There were still three days to go, when he heard voices from next door. A woman was calling in the garden. 'Alex! Dinner's ready.'

He was surprised at the lift in his heart. Alex was there. He gave them an hour to eat their dinner, then he rang Mr Jenkins's front door bell.

He had never before seen the woman who answered it. She was small and, he couldn't help admitting, pretty. Not at all like Alex to look at, but when she spoke, her voice was just like her daughter's.

'Yes?'

145

'I wondered if I could see Alex?'

She said, 'Are you Stephen from next door?' When he said, 'Yes,' she turned into the hall and called, 'Alex! It's your friend Stephen.' Turning back, she said, 'Alex doesn't know anyone else here. That's how I guessed it was you.'

Remembering his manners, he said, 'I hope you had a good Christmas.'

'It was all right. I'm not that keen on Christmases. They're fun when you've got little kids, but not so much when you're all nearly grown up.'

Sensible woman. Would his mum be as calm about anniversaries as this? Alex appeared behind her mother and said, 'Hi!'

'Hi!'

Alex's mother stepped back and disappeared. Alex and Stephen stood looking at each other.

'I can't ask you in,' Alex said.

'That's all right.' Stephen considered the possibilities of his own house. Dad was in the kitchen, either sleeping or watching television. He said, 'Come for a walk?'

She looked pleased. 'I'll get my coat.'

He waited until she reappeared in a short thick coat which was too large for her. She laughed when she saw his look. 'One of my Christmas presents. It's miles too big, but it's really warm.'

They walked through the overgrown garden. 'Where'll we go?'

'The park?'

'It'll be full of kids learning to ride their new bikes.'

'I don't mind.'

When they had found a bench among a little maze of paths too rough for the bike learners, Alex asked, 'Did you have a nice Christmas?'

'Not really. Did you?'

146

'I quite liked it. I got some really good presents. Did you get anything exciting?'

'My dad gave me a computer game. Trouble is, we haven't got a computer.'

'So how'll you play it?'

'One of my friends's got one. I'll go round to his house and we'll play there.'

'Anything else? Present, I mean?'

He told her about his gran's old purse and Aunt Alice's postal order. 'It's good of her, because she hasn't any money. But the chicken she cooked was terrible. I had to swallow it in gobbets so as not to taste it.'

'That's bad. I'm lucky. My mum's a super cook.'

Stephen wondered whether his mum could cook. Perhaps she'd forgotten how to. He didn't know if a prisoner could cook in prison.

Alex said, doubtfully, 'Steve?'

'What?'

'Did you get to see your mum?'

He was half glad that she'd brought the subject up. 'Yes.'

'Would you rather not talk about it?'

'I don't mind. I just saw her. Not to talk to or anything.'

'Was it with one of your keys?'

'Yes.'

'What did it feel like?'

'Peculiar.'

'Is she like what you thought?'

'No. She's . . . ' He sought for the right words. 'She's more ordinary.'

'Do you mind?'

'No.'

'Did you remember her at all?'

'No.'

'When are you going to see her properly? To talk to?'

'She's coming out in the New Year. In another three days. But not here. She's staying somewhere else at first.'

Alex considered this for a little, before she said, 'I can't imagine what it'd be like to have a mum I'd never seen. I mean, couldn't remember.'

There seemed nothing to say to this.

'I'm sorry. I shouldn't have said that,' Alex said.

'It's all right. I don't know what it's going to be like either.'

'I hope you'll like each other.'

What an extraordinary thing to say! Stephen asked, 'What do you mean, "like"?'

'You know. Really like. Think you're interesting. Think the same things are funny. Not annoying. *Like*. Like I like you.'

He was embarrassed. He said, 'Aren't you getting cold?'

She laughed. 'All right. I know what you're thinking. It's time you took the girl back and stopped her asking questions, and saying stupid things.'

They started back. They hardly exchanged a word. When they reached old Mr Jenkins's garden gate, Alex said, 'I hope everything's all right for you.'

'Thanks.'

'We'll probably be back here some time. Half term perhaps. You'll be here then?'

'Expect so.'

'Can I ask you something?'

He said, 'Suppose so.' Reluctant.

'It's about your keys.'

'Go on.'

'Have you tried them all now?'

'Yes.'

'So what are you going to do with them?'

He hadn't thought. 'They won't be any more use. There won't be any keyholes for them.'

'How do you know? You can't be sure about that.'

He told her how the keyhole in the garden door, into which the Yale with a face had fitted, had changed.

'So I reckon the other locks will have gone too.'

'Shall we have a look some time? To make sure?'

'If you like. But I'll bet you they won't be there.'

'Bet me how much?'

'I'll give you the key that fits if there is one.'

'I don't think it would work for me,' Alex said.

'Why not?' But he didn't believe it would either. They were his keys. They had opened the doors for him. They would do nothing for anyone else.

'Well, anyway, Happy New Year. For next week.'

'Same to you.'

'Bye!'

'Bye.'

24

Stephen met the woman who had been his mother in a room that struck him as too bright, too cheerful, too clean. A room that didn't belong to anyone. The woman he had seen with her by the leaded gate had let him and his dad into the house and left them here together.

He couldn't look at her. He kept his eyes fixed on the too-flowery carpet. He heard his dad say, 'I've brought the boy,' and her voice answer. When she said, 'Hi, Stephen!' he muttered something, but he didn't look up. They all sat down, stiff, on the edge of cretonne-covered chairs. He heard those two making uncomfortable, unreal conversation. He could tell from their voices that they were not really interested in what they were saying. Each of them was thinking quite differently. Then suddenly, the woman laughed. She said, 'Give up, Will. We don't want to go on like this. You go and talk to Petra. She's in the kitchen making coffee. Stephen and I need to be alone for a bit.'

She went to the door and called out, 'Petra! I'm sending Will to talk to you for a bit. Don't send him back too soon.'

Stephen had never heard anyone order his dad about like that, and he was surprised that he went so meekly. As the door closed behind him, Stephen's heart sank. Now this woman would get soppy. She would call him Deedie, she would expect him to kiss her. She would ask if he remembered her. Probably she would cry over him and say how she had missed him.

He was relieved when she sat down where she had been before, at some distance. He knew she was looking at him. Presently she said, 'It isn't easy, is it? Getting to know each other?'

He said, 'No.'

'I think you should call me by my name. It seems stupid if you start saying "Mum" after all these years.'

He was surprised into saying, 'You mean call you Margaret?'

'Why not?'

'Seems funny.'

'Don't any of your friends call their parents by their given names?'

He had to think. 'Only if they're steps.'

'I'm not much more than a step, am I? I couldn't be more of a stranger.'

Good. She wasn't expecting him to behave as if she'd been his mother for ever.

There was a silence, but it wasn't as uncomfortable. Suddenly she said, 'Don't you want to ask me any questions?'

He was wary at once. 'What about?'

'Anything you like.'

'Really anything?'

'Anything at all. I might say I wouldn't tell you, but I don't mind you asking. I know I'd want to if I was you.'

The most important question came first. 'Are you going to come and live with us?'

'I can't answer that because I don't know. Will and I haven't seen much of each other in the last eight years. It's a long time. I don't know how we'd get on now.' And there's me, Stephen thought. As if she'd heard him, she said, 'And there's you.'

'What about me?'

151

'You're old enough now to have opinions of your own. It might not suit you to have a mother come back from the dead.' She laughed. 'Well, as good as dead. I suppose we'd have to tell the neighbours I'd been with my sisters in Australia.'

'You mean, if I didn't want you to come back, you wouldn't?' he said.

'It would be something we'd certainly take into account.'

She was quite different from what he'd expected. She was treating him as if he was grown up. Sensible. That made him feel better about her.

She was saying, 'I'd probably try to win you round, if it came to that.'

He wondered how she would do it. The suggestion made him suspicious again. He would test her. She had said he could ask anything he liked. He said, 'What's it like, being in prison?'

She did not baulk at that. 'Fairly horrible at first. Then you begin to get used to it.'

'Used to what?'

'Having people round you all the time. Being watched always.'

Yes. He could imagine that. He said, 'Did you mind not being able to get out?'

She said, 'Of course. That's part of the punishment, isn't it?'

There was no need to answer this. She was looking hard at him now. She said, 'Go on!'

'Go on what?'

'You want to ask me what it's like to have done what I did. Kill someone.'

He had wanted to, but hadn't known how. He said, 'What is it like, then?'

'Terrible. You can't believe you've really done it.' She

stopped speaking for a moment, then said, 'But I'm not sorry. I'd do it again. If I had to.'

'Did you have to?'

She looked at him strangely. She said, 'The man I killed had tried to ruin my life. I wasn't having him doing it again. To me and then to someone else as well.'

'What did he do?'

She said, 'I'm afraid that's a question I'm not going to answer till I know you better.'

He wondered when that would be. He still wanted to push, to get at her somehow. 'You said he tried to ruin your life. Why didn't he manage to do it?'

'He did for a time.'

'What happened then?'

Her expression changed. She said, 'I met Will.'

'Dad?' Stephen asked, astonished.

'Your dad.'

'What did he do?'

She said, quietly, 'He loved me.'

He was so surprised that he said, without meaning to, 'Did he say so?'

She laughed. 'You've lived with your dad all these years and you don't know the answer to that?'

Of course he did. But then, how had she known? And now she had mentioned the word love, he wasn't as embarrassed as he'd have expected. At least, she hadn't asked him to love her. She was prepared to be treated as a stranger.

She said, 'I know it's difficult for you, meeting me. But it isn't easy for me either.'

'Isn't it?'

She was impatient. 'For Christ's sake, think! You can't be so young that you really suppose that being grown up means that you always know what to do whatever's going on? What do you think it's like for me, meeting a son I

153

haven't seen since he was a baby? Or a husband I've only seen once a month for eight years? I don't know what sort of a person either of you's turned into while I've been inside. I don't even know if I'm going to like you. Or whether you'll like me.'

She was right. He hadn't thought about her feelings. He had only wondered how this meeting was going to turn out for him. He said, 'I'm sorry.'

'That's all right. I just wanted you to know.'

She got up and went to the door. She called out, 'Petra! Will! You can bring in that coffee now.'

She came back to her chair and said to Stephen, 'It's going to take time.'

'What's going to take time? What for?'

'Time to find out how we get on with each other. We'll start from scratch, as if we'd never known each other, that'll be the best way. But there's no hurry. Not for me.'

He had time, before Petra and his dad came back into the room with mugs of coffee and a plate of biscuits, to say, 'I'm not in a hurry either.'

She smiled at him, then. He remembered what Alex had said. 'I hope you like each other.' She hadn't said 'love'. Was it possible that liking was as important as loving? That was not what you were supposed to learn from books and films and television programmes. It was a strange idea. It was as strange as hearing this woman say that his dad had loved her. So love came into it somewhere, he wasn't sure where. He had been mad at the idea that he would be expected to love this strange woman who had once been his mother, but now he did begin to feel that possibly he might get to like her. In the future, which lay, uncharted, before them.